MARIE,

A Story of Russian Love

ALEXANDER PUSHKIN

Translated by Marie H. de Zielinska

1st WORLD
LIBRARY
Literary Society

Marie

Alexander Pushkin

© 1st World Library, 2009
PO Box 2211
Fairfield, IA 52556
www.1stworldlibrary.com
First Edition

LCCN: 2009923325

Softcover ISBN: 978-1-4218-8802-6
Hardcover ISBN: 978-1-4218-8901-6
eBook ISBN: 978-1-4218-8703-6

Purchase *"Marie"*
as a traditional bound book at:
www.1stWorldLibrary.com/purchase.asp?ISBN=978-1-4218-8802-6

1st World Library is a literary, educational organization
dedicated to:

- Creating a free internet library of downloadable ebooks

- Hosting writing competitions and offering book publishing
scholarships.

Interested in more 1st World Library books? contact:
literacy@1stworldlibrary.com
Check us out at: www.1stworldlibrary.com

1st World Library Literary Society

Giving Back to the World

"If you want to work on the core problem, it's early school literacy."

- James Barksdale, former CEO of Netscape

"No skill is more crucial to the future of a child, or to a democratic and prosperous society, than literacy."

- Los Angeles Times

"Literacy... means far more than learning how to read and write... The aim is to transmit... knowledge and promote social participation."

- UNESCO

"Literacy is not a luxury, it is a right and a responsibility. If our world is to meet the challenges of the twenty-first century we must harness the energy and creativity of all our citizens."

- President Bill Clinton

"Parents should be encouraged to read to their children, and teachers should be equipped with all available techniques for teaching literacy, so the varying needs and capacities of individual kids can be taken into account."

- Hugh Mackay

CONTENTS

TRANSLATOR'S NOTE

Alexander Pushkin, the most distinguished poet of Russia, was born at Saint Petersburg, 1799. When only twenty-one years of age he entered the civil service in the department of foreign affairs. Lord Byron's writings and efforts for Greek independence exercised great influence over Pushkin, whose "Ode to Liberty" cost him his freedom. He was exiled to Bessarabia [A region of Moldova and western Ukraine] from 1820 to 1825, whence he returned at the accession of the new emperor, Nicholas, who made him historiographer of Peter the Great. Pushkin's friends now looked upon him as a traitor to the cause of liberty. It is not improbable that an enforced residence at the mouth of the Danube somewhat cooled his patriotic enthusiasm. Every Autumn, his favorite season for literary production, he usually passed at his country seat in the province Pekoff. Here from 1825 to 1829 he published "Pultowa," "Boris Godunoff," "Eugene Onegin," and "Ruslaw and Ludmila," a tale in verse, after the Manner of Ariosto's "Orlando Furioso." This is considered as the first great poetical work in the Russian language, though the critics of the day attacked it, because it was beyond their grasp; but the public devoured it.

In 1831 Pushkin married, and soon after appeared his charming novel, "Marie," a picture of garrison life on the

Russian plains. Peter and Marie of this Northern story are as pure as their native snows, and whilst listening to the recital, we inhale the odor of the steppe, and catch glimpses of the semi-barbarous Kalmouk and the Cossack of the Don.

A duel with his brother-in-law terminated the life of Pushkin in the splendor of his talent. The emperor munificently endowed the poet's family, and ordered a superb edition of all his works to be published at the expense of the crown. His death was mourned by his countrymen as a national calamity.

M. H. de Z.

Chicago, Nov. 1, 1876.

I

THE SERGEANT OF THE GUARDS

My father, Andrew Peter Grineff, having served in his youth under Count Munich, left the army in 17—, with the grade of First Major. From that time he lived on his estate in the Principality of Simbirsk, where he married Avoditia, daughter of a poor noble in the neighborhood. Of nine children, the issue of this marriage, I was the only survivor. My brothers and sisters died in childhood.

Through the favor of a near relative of ours, Prince B—, himself a Major in the Guards, I was enrolled Sergeant of the Guards in the regiment of Semenofski. It was understood that I was on furlough till my education should be finished. From my fifth year I was confided to the care of an old servant Saveliitch, whose steadiness promoted him to the rank of my personal attendant. Thanks to his care, when I was twelve years of age I knew how to read and write, and could make a correct estimate of the points of a hunting dog.

At this time, to complete my education, my father engaged upon a salary a Frenchman, M. Beaupre, who was brought from Moscow with one year's provision of wine and oil from Provence. His arrival of course displeased Saveliitch.

Beaupre had been in his own country a valet, in Prussia a soldier, then he came to Russia to be a tutor, not knowing very well what the word meant in our language. He was a good fellow, astonishingly gay and absent-minded. His chief foible was a passion for the fair sex. Nor was he, to use his own expression, an enemy to the bottle —that is to say, *a la Russe*, he loved drink. But as at home wine was offered only at table, and then in small glasses, and as, moreover, on these occasions, the servants passed by the pedagogue, Beaupre soon accustomed himself to Russian brandy, and, in time, preferred it, as a better tonic, to the wines of his native country. We became great friends, and although according to contract he was engaged to teach me French, German, and *all the sciences*, yet he was content that I should teach him to chatter Russian. But as each of us minded his own business, our friendship was constant, and I desired no mentor. However, destiny very soon separated us, in consequence of an event which I will relate.

Our laundress, a fat girl all scarred by small-pox, and our dairymaid, who was blind of an eye, agreed, one fine day, to throw themselves at my mother's feet and accuse the Frenchman of trifling with their innocence and inexperience!

My mother would have no jesting upon this point, and she in turn complained to my father, who, like a man of business, promptly ordered "that dog of a Frenchman" into his presence. The servant informed him meekly that Beaupre was at the moment engaged in giving me a lesson.

My father rushed to my room. Beaupre was sleeping upon his bed the sleep of innocence. I was deep in a most interesting occupation. They had brought from Moscow, for me, a geographical map, which hung unused against the wall; the width and strength of its paper had been to me a standing temptation. I had determined to make a kite of it, and profiting that morning by Beaupre's sleep, I had set to work. My father came in just as I was tying a tail to the Cape of Good Hope! Seeing my work, he seized me by the ear and shook me soundly; then rushing to Beaupre's bed, awakened him without hesitating, pouring forth a volley of abuse upon the head of the unfortunate Frenchman. In his confusion Beaupre tried in vain to rise; the poor pedagogue was dead drunk! My father caught him by the coat-collar and flung him out of the room. That day he was dismissed, to the inexpressible delight of Saveliitch.

Thus ended my education. I now lived in the family as the eldest son, not of age whose career is yet to open; amusing myself teaching pigeons to tumble on the roof, and playing leap-frog in the stable- yard with the grooms. In this way I reached my sixteenth year.

One Autumn day, my mother was preserving fruit with honey in the family room, and I, smacking my lips, was looking at the liquid boiling; my father, seated near the window, had just opened the *Court Almanac* which he received every year. This book had great influence over him; he read it with extreme attention, and reading prodigiously stirred up his bile. My mother, knowing by heart all his ways and oddities, used to try to hide the miserable book, and often whole months would pass without a sight of it. But, in revenge whenever he did happen to find it, he would sit for hours with the book before his eyes.

Well, my father was reading the *Court Almanac,*

frequently shrugging his shoulders, and murmuring: "'General!' Umph, he was a sergeant in my company. 'Knight of the Orders of Russia.' Can it be so long since we—?"

Finally he flung the *Almanac* away on the sofa and plunged into deep thought; a proceeding that never presaged anything good.

"Avoditia," said he, brusquely, to my mother, "how old is Peter?"

"His seventeenth precious year has just begun," said my mother. "Peter was born the year Aunt Anastasia lost her eye, and that was—"

"Well, well," said my father, "it is time he should join the army. It is high time he should give up his nurse, leap-frog and pigeon training."

The thought of a separation so affected my poor mother that she let the spoon fall into the preserving pan, and tears rained from her eyes.

As for me, it is difficult to express my joy. The idea of army service was mingled in my head with that of liberty, and the pleasures offered by a great city like Saint Petersburg. I saw myself an officer in the Guards, which, in my opinion was the height of felicity.

As my father neither liked to change his plans, nor delay their execution, the day of my departure was instantly fixed. That evening, saying that he would give me a letter to my future chief, he called for writing materials.

"Do not forget, Andrew," said my mother, "to salute for

me Prince B. Tell him that I depend upon his favor for my darling Peter."

"What nonsense," said my father, frowning, "why should I write to Prince B.?"

"You have just said that you would write to Peter's future chief."

"Well, what then?"

"Prince B. is his chief. You know very well that Peter is enrolled in the Semenofski regiment."

"Enrolled! what's that to me? Enrolled or not enrolled, he shall not go to Saint Petersburg. What would he learn there? Extravagance and folly. No! let him serve in the army, let him smell powder, let him be a soldier and not a do-nothing in the Guards; let him wear the straps of his knapsack out. Where is the certificate of his birth and baptism?"

My mother brought the certificate, which she kept in a little box with my baptismal robe, and handed it to my father. He read it, placed it before him on the table, and commenced his letter.

I was devoured by curiosity. Where am I going, thought I, if not to Saint Petersburg? I did not take my eyes from the pen which my father moved slowly across the paper.

At last, the letter finished, he put it and my certificate under the same envelope, took off his spectacles, called me and said:

"This letter is addressed to Andrew Karlovitch, my old

friend and comrade. You are going to Orenbourg to serve under orders."

All my brilliant dreams vanished. In place of the gay life of Saint Petersburg, ennui awaited me in a wild and distant province of the empire. Military life seemed now a calamity.

The next morning a kibitka was at the door; my trunk was placed on it, and also a case holding tea and a tea-service, with some napkins full of rolls and pastry, the last sweet bits of the paternal home. Both my parents gave me their solemn benediction. My father said, "Adieu, Peter. Serve faithfully him to whom your oath is given; obey your chiefs; neither seek favor, nor solicit service, but do not reject them; and remember the proverb: 'Take care of thy coat whilst it is new, and thy honor whilst it is fresh.'"

My darling mother, all in tears, told me to take care of my health; and counseled Saveliitch to guard her child from danger.

I was wrapped up in a short touloup lined with hare-skin, and over that a pelisse lined fox-skin. I took my seat in the kibitka with Saveliitch, and shedding bitter tears, set out for my destination.

That night I arrived at Simbirsk, where I was to stay twenty-four hours, in order that Saveliitch might make various purchases entrusted to him. Early in the morning Saveliitch went to the shops, whilst I stayed in the inn. Tired of gazing out of the window upon a dirty little street, I rambled about the inn, and at last entered the billiard-room. I found there a tall gentleman, some forty years of age, with heavy black moustaches, in his dressing-gown, holding a cue and smoking his pipe. He was playing with the marker, who was to drink a glass of brandy and water if he gained, and if he lost was to pass, on all-fours, under the billiard table. I watched them playing. The more they played the more frequent became the promenades on all-fours, so that finally the marker stayed under the table. The gentleman pronounced over him some energetic expression, as a funeral oration, and then proposed that I should play a game with him. I declared that I did not know how to play billiards. That seemed strange to him. He looked at me with commiseration.

However, we opened a conversation. I learned that his name was Ivan Zourine; that he was a chief of a squadron of Hussars stationed then at Simbirsk recruiting soldiers, and that his quarters were at my inn. He invited me to mess with him, soldier-fashion, pot-luck. I accepted with pleasure, and we sat down to dinner. Zourine drank deeply, and invited me to drink also, saying that I must become accustomed to the service. He told stories of garrison life which made me laugh till I held my sides, and we rose from the table intimate friends. He then proposed to teach me how to play billiards. "It is," said he, "indispensable for soldiers like ourselves. For example, suppose we arrive in a town, what's to be done? We can not always make sport of the Jews. As a last resort there is the inn and the billiard-room; but to play billiards, one must know how." These reasons convinced me, and I set about learning with enthusiasm.

Zourine encouraged me in a loud tone; he was astonished at my rapid progress, and after a few lesson he proposed to play for money, were it only two kopecks, not for the gain, merely to avoid playing for nothing, which was, according to him, a very bad habit. I agreed. Zourine ordered punch, which he advised me to taste in order to become used to the service, "for," said he, "what kind of service would that be without punch?"

I took his advice, and we continued to play; the more I tasted of my glass the bolder I grew. I made the balls fly over the cushions; I was angry with the marker who was counting. Heaven knows why. I increased the stake, and behaved, altogether, like a boy just cut free, for the first time, from his mother's apron-strings. The time passed quickly. At last, Zourine glanced at the clock, laid down his cue, and said that I had lost a hundred roubles to him.

I was in great confusion, because my money was all in the hands of Saveliitch. I began to mumble excuses, when Zourine exclaimed, "Oh! well! Good God! I can wait till morning; don't be distressed about it. Now let us go to supper." What could I do? I finished the day as foolishly as I began it.

Zourine never ceased pouring out drinks for me; advising me to become accustomed to the service. Rising from table, I could scarcely stand. At midnight Zourine brought me back to the inn.

Saveliitch met us at the door, and uttered a cry of horror when he saw the unmistakable signs of my "zeal for the service."

"What has happened to thee?" said he, in heart-broken accents; "where have you been filling yourself like a sack? Oh! heavenly father! a misfortune like this never came before."

"Silence! old owl," said I, stammering, "I am sure you are drunk yourself; go to bed, but first put me there."

Alexander Pushkin

I awoke next morning with a severe headache; the events of the evening I recalled vaguely, but my recollections became vivid at the sight of Saveliitch who came to me with a cup of tea.

"You begin young, Peter Grineff," said the old men, shaking his head. "Eh! from whom do you inherit it? Neither your father nor grandfather were drunkards. Your mother's name can not be mentioned; she never deigned to taste any thing but cider. Whose fault is it then? That cursed Frenchman's; he taught three fine things, that miserable dog—that pagan—for thy teacher, as if his lordship, thy father, had not people of his own."

I was ashamed before the old man; I turned my face away saying, "I do not want any tea, go away, Saveliitch." It was not easy to stop Saveliitch, once he began to preach.

"Now, Peter, you see what it is to play the fool. You have a headache, you have no appetite, a drunkard is good for nothing. Here, take some of this decoction of cucumber and honey, or half a glass of brandy to sober you. What do you say to that?"

At that instant a boy entered the room with a note for me from Zourine. I unfolded it and read as follows:

"Do me the favor, my dear Peter, to send me by my servant the hundred roubles that you lost to me yesterday. I am horribly in want of money. Your devoted. ZOURINE."

As I was perfectly in his power, I assumed an air of indifference, and ordered Saveliitch to give a hundred roubles to the boy.

"What? why?" said the old man, surprised.

"I owe that sum," said I, coolly.

"You owe it? When had you time enough to contract such a debt?" said he, with redoubled astonishment. "No, no, that's impossible. Do what you like, my lord, but I can not give the money."

I reflected that if in this decisive moment I did not oblige the obstinate old fellow to obey me, it would be impossible in the future to escape from his tutelage. Looking at him therefore, haughtily, I said, "I am thy master; thou art my servant. The money is mine, and I lost because I chose to lose it; I advise thee to obey when ordered, and not assume the airs of a master."

My words affected Saveliitch so much that he clasped his hands and stood bowed down mute and motionless.

"What are you doing there like a post?" I cried out, angrily.

Saveliitch was in tears.

"Oh! my dear master Peter," stammered he, with trembling voice, "do not kill me with grief. Oh my light, listen to me, an old man; write to that brigand that you were jesting, that we never had so much money. A hundred roubles! God of goodness! Tell him thy parents strictly forbade thee to play for any thing but nuts."

"Silence," said I, with severity, "give the money or I'll chase you out of the room."

Saveliitch looked at me with agony, and went for the money. I pitied the good old man, but I wanted to emancipate myself, and prove that I was no longer a child.

Saveliitch sent the money to Zourine, and then hastened our departure from that cursed inn.

I left Simbirsk with a troubled conscience; a secret remorse oppressed me. I took no leave of my teacher, not dreaming that I should ever meet him again.

II

THE GUIDE

My reflections during the journey were not very agreeable. According to the value of money at that time my loss was of some importance. I could not but admit to myself that my conduct at the inn at Simbirsk had been very silly, and I felt guilty toward Saveliitch. The old man was seated on the front of the vehicle in dull silence; from time to time turning his head and coughing a cough of ill humor. I had firmly resolved to make friends with him, but I did not know which way to begin. At last I said to him, "Come, come Saveliitch, let us put an end to this; I know I was wrong; I was a fool yesterday, and offended you without cause, but I promise to listen to you in future. Come, do not be angry, let us make friends!"

"Ah! My dear Peter," said he with a sigh, "I am angry with myself. It's I who was wrong in every thing. How could I have left you alone at the inn? How could it have been avoided? The devil had a hand in it! I wanted to go and see the deacon's wife, who is my god-mother, and as the proverb says: 'I left the house and fell into the prison.'"

What a misfortune! what a misfortune! How can I appear before the eyes of my masters? What will they say, when

Alexander Pushkin

they shall hear that their child is a drunkard and a gambler. To console dear old Saveliitch, I gave him my word, that for the future I would not dispose of single kopeck without his consent. Little by little he became calm, which did not, however, prevent him from grumbling out, now and then shaking his head: "A hundred roubles! It is easy to talk!"

I drew near the place of my destination. Around me extended a desert, sad and wild, broken be little hills and deep ravines, all covered with snow. The sun was setting.

My kibitka followed the narrow road, or rather trace, left by peasants' sledges. Suddenly my coachman, looking at a certain point and addressing me, "My lord," said he, taking off his cap, "do you not command us to retrace our steps?"

"What for?"

"The weather is uncertain. There is some wind ahead; do you see it drive the snow on the surface?"

"What matter?"

"And do you not see what is over yonder?" pointing with his whip to the east.

"I see nothing more than the white steppes and the clear sky."

"There! there! that little cloud!"

I saw indeed upon the horizon a little white cloud that I had at first taken for a distant hill. My coachman explained to me that this little cloud foretold a *chasse-neige*—a snowdrift. I had heard of the drifting snows of this region, and I know that at times, storms swallowed up whole caravans. Saveliitch agreed with the coachman, and advised our return.

But to me the wind did not seem very strong. I hoped to arrive in time for the next relay of horses. I gave orders, therefore, to redouble our speed. The coachman put his horses to the gallop, and kept his eyes to the east.

The wind blew harder and harder. The little cloud soon became a great white mass, rising heavily, growing, extending, and finally invading the whole sky. A fine snow began to fall, which suddenly changed to immense flakes. The wind whistled and howled. It was a *chasse-neige*—a snowdrift.

In an instant the somber sky was confounded with the sea of snow which the wind raised up from the earth. Every thing was indistinguishable.

"Woe, to us! my lord," cried the coachman, "it is a whirlwind of snow!"

I put my head out of the kibitka—darkness and storm. The wind blew with an expression so ferocious that it seemed a living creature.

The snow fell in large flakes upon us, covering us. The horses went at a walking pace, but very soon stood still.

"Why do you not go on?" I said to the coachman.

"Go where?" he replied, as he got down from the kibitka. "God knows where we are now! There is no road; all is darkness."

I began to scold him. Saveliitch took up his defense:

"Why did you not listen to him," said he, angrily; "you could have returned, taken some tea and slept till morning; the storm would have been over, and we could then have set out. Why this haste? as if you were going to your wedding?"

Saveliitch was right. What was to be done? The snow continued to fall; it was heaped up around the kibitka; the horses stood motionless, now and then shivering. The coachman walked around them adjusting their harness, as if he had nothing else to do.

Saveliitch grumbled.

I strained my eyes in every direction, hoping to see signs of a dwelling, or of a road, but I could only see the whirling of the snow-drift. All at once I thought I saw some thing black. "Halloo! coachman," I cried out, "what is that black thing yonder?"

The coachman looked attentively where I indicated. "God knows, my lord," he replied, re-mounting to his seat; "it is not a kibitka, nor a tree; it seems to be moving. It must be a wolf or a man!"

I ordered him to go in the direction of the unknown object which was coming toward us. In two minutes we were on a line with it, and I recognized a man.

"Halloo! good man!" shouted my coachman; "tell us, do you know the road?"

"This is the road," replied the man. "I am on solid ground, but what the devil is the good of that."

"Listen, my good peasant," said I; "do you know this country? Can you lead us to a shelter for the night?"

"This country! Thank God, I have been over it on foot and in carriage, from one end to the other. But one can not help losing the road in this weather. It is better to stop here and wait till the hurricane ceases: then the sky will clear, and we can find the way by the stars."

His coolness gave me courage. I had decided to trust myself to the mercy of God and pass the night on the steppe, when the traveler, seating himself on the bench which was the coachman's seat, said to the driver:

"Thank God, a dwelling is near. Turn to the right and go on."

"Why should I turn to the right?" said the coachman, sulkily, "where do you see a road?"

"Must I say to you these horses, as well as the harness, belong to another? then use the whip without respite."

I thought my coachman's view rational.

"Why do you believe," said I to the new-comer, "that a dwelling is not far off?"

"The wind blows from that quarter," said he, "and I have smelled smoke—proof that a dwelling is near."

His sagacity, the delicacy of his sense of smell, filled me with admiration; I ordered my coachman to go wherever the other wished. The horses walked heavily through the deep snow. The kibitka advanced but slowly, now raised on a hillock, now descending into a hollow, swaying from side like a boat on a stormy sea.

Saveliitch, falling over on me every instant, moaned. I pulled down the hood of the kibitka, wrapped myself up in my pelisse, and fell asleep, rocked by the swaying of the vehicle, and lulled by the chant of the tempest.

The horses stopped. Saveliitch was holding my hand.

"Come out, my lord," said he, "we have arrived."

"Where have we arrived?" said I, rubbing my eyes.

"At the shelter. God has helped us; we have stumbled right upon the hedge of the dwelling. Come out, my lord, quick; come and warm yourself."

I descended from the kibitka; the hurricane had not ceased, but it had moderated; sight was useless, it was so dark. The master of the house met us at the door, holding a lantern under the flaps of his long coat, the Cossack cafetan. He led us into a small, though no untidy room, lighted by a pine torch. In the centre hung a carabine and a high Cossack cap.

Our host, a Cossack from the river Iaik, was a peasant of some sixty years, still fresh and green.

Saveliitch brought in the case containing my tea-service; he asked for fire to make me a few cups of tea, of which I never had greater need. The host hastened to serve us.

"Where is our guide?" I asked of Saveliitch.

"Here, your lordship," replied a voice from above. I raised my eyes to the loft, and saw a black beard and two sparkling black eyes.

"Well, are you cold?"

"How could I help being cold in this little cafetan full of holes. What's the use of concealment? I had a touloup, but I left it yesterday in pledge with the liquor-seller; then the cold did not seem so great."

At this moment our host entered with the portable furnace and boiler, the Russian *Somovar*. I offered our guide a cup of tea. Down he came at once. As he stood in the glare of the pine torch his appearance was remarkable. A man about forty years of age, medium height, slight but with broad shoulders. His black beard was turning grey; large, quick, restless eyes, gave him an expression full of cunning, and yet not at all disagreeable. He was dressed in wide Tartar pantaloons and an old jacket. His hair was cut evenly round.

I offered him a cup of tea. He tasted it and made a grimace.

"Do me the favor, my lord, to order me a glass of brandy; tea is not the Cossack's drink."

I willingly granted the request. The host took from the shelf of a closet a bottle and a glass, and going up to him, looking him full in the face, said:

"Ah! ah! here you are again in our district. Whence has God brought you?"

My guide winked in the most significant fashion and replied by the well-know proverb: The sparrow was in the orchard eating flax-seed; the grandmother threw a stone at it, and missed. "And you? how are all yours?"

"How are we?" said the host, and continuing in proverbs: "They began to ring the bell for Vespers, but the priest's wife forbade it. The priest went visiting, and the devils are in the graveyard."

"Be silent, uncle," said the vagabond.

"When there shall be rain, there will be mushrooms, and when there shall be mushrooms, there will be a basket to put them in. Put thy hatchet behind thy back, the forest guard is out walking."

"To your lordship's health." Taking the glass, he made the sign of the cross, and at one gulp swallowed his brandy. He then saluted me and remounted to his loft. I did not understand a word of this thief's slang. It was only in the sequel that I learned that they spoke of the affairs of the army of the Iaik, which had just been reduced to obedience after the revolt of 1772. Saveliitch listened and glanced suspiciously from host to guide.

The species of inn where we were sheltered was in the very heart of the steppes, far from the road and every inhabited spot, and looked very much like a rendezvous of robbers. But to set off again on our journey was impossible. The disgust of Saveliitch amused not a little; however, he finally decided to mount upon the roof of the stove, the ordinary bed of the Russian peasant. The warm bricks of the hot-air chamber of the stove diffused a grateful heat, and soon the old man and the host, who had laid himself on the floor, were snoring. I stretched myself upon a bench, and slept like a dead. Awaking next morning quite late, I saw that the hurricane was over. The sun shone out, the snow extended in the distance like a sheet of dazzling white damask. The horses were already at the door, harnessed. I paid our host, who asked so small a pittance that even Saveliitch did not, as usual, haggle over the price. His suspicions of the evening before had entirely disappeared. I called the guide to thank him for the service he had done us, and told Saveliitch to give him half a rouble. Saveliitch frowned.

"Half a rouble," said he; "What for? Because you yourself deigned to bring him to the inn? Your will be done, my lord, but we have not a rouble to spare. If we begin by giving drink money to every one we shall end by dying of hunger."

It was useless to argue with him; my money, according to my promise, was entirely at his discretion. But it was very unpleasant not to be able to reward a man who had extricated me from danger, perhaps death.

"Well," said I, coolly, "if you will not give him half a rouble, give one of my coats—he is too thinly clad; give him the hare- skin touloup."

"Have mercy on me! My dear Peter," said Saveliitch, "what does he want with your touloup? He will drink its price, the dog, at the first inn."

"That, my good old man, is none of your business," said the vagabond; "his lordship following the custom of royalty to vassals, gives me a coat from his own back, and your duty as serf is not to dispute, but to obey."

"You have not the fear of God, brigand that you are," said Saveliitch, angrily; "you see that the child has not yet attained to full reason, and there you are, glad to pillage him, thanks to his kind heart. You can not even wear the pelisse on your great, cursed shoulders."

"Come," said I, "do not play the logician; bring the touloup quickly."

"Oh, Lord!" said the old man, moaning—"a touloup of hare-skin! Quite new,—to give it to a drunkard in rags."

It was brought, however, and the vagabond began to get into it. It was rather tight for me, and was much too small for him. He put it on, nevertheless, but with great difficulty, bursting all the seams. Saveliitch uttered something like a smothered howl, when he heard the threads crack. As for the vagabond, he was well pleased with my present. He re-conducted me to my kibitka, and said, with a profound bow: "Thanks, my lord, may god reward you. I shall never forget your goodness."

He went his way,—I set out on mine, paying no attention to the sullenness of Saveliitch. I soon forgot the hurricane and the guide, as well as the touloup of hare-skin.

Arrived at Orenbourg, I presented myself at once to the General. He was a tall man, bent by age, with long hair quite white. An old, worn-out uniform, recalled the soldier of the times of the Empress Anne, and his speech betrayed a strong German accent.

I gave him my father's letter.

Reading my name, he glanced at me quickly. "Mein Gott," said he, "it is so short a time since Andrew Grineff was your age, and now, see what a fine fellow of a son he has. Ah! time! time!" He opened the letter and began to run it over with a commentary of remarks.

"'Sir, I hope your Excellency,'—What is this; what is the meaning of this ceremony? discipline, of course before all, but is this the way to write to an old friend? Hum—'Field-marshal Munich—little Caroline—brother.' Ah! then he remembers—'Now to business. I send you my son; hold him with porcupine gloves.'

"What does that mean?" said he, "that must be a Russian proverb."

"It means," said I, with an air of innocence, "to treat a person mildly, to give one liberty."

"Hum!" said he, reading, "'and give him no liberty.' No," he continued, "your proverb does not mean liberty. Well, my son," said he, having finished the letter, "every thing shall be done for you. You shall be an officer in the— regiment, and not to lose time, go tomorrow to the fort of Belogorsk, where you will serve under Captain Mironoff, a brave and honest man. There you will see service and learn discipline. You have nothing to do here at Orenbourg, and amusements are dangerous to a young man. Today I invite you to dine with me."

From bad to worse, thought I. What was the use of being a Sergeant in the Guards almost from my mother's womb? To what has it led? To the regiment of—, and an abandoned fortress on the frontier of the steppes!

I dined at the General's in company with his old Aid-de-camp. Severe German economy reigned at table, and I think the fear of having an occasional guest the more had something to do with sending me to a distant garrison.

The next day I took my leave of the General and set out for Belogorsk.

III

THE FORTRESS

The fortress of Belogorsk is situated forty versts from Orenbourg. The route from this city is along the high banks of the river Iaik. The stream was not yet frozen, and its lead-colored waters took a black tint between banks whitened by the snow. Before me lay the Kirghis steppes. I fell into a moody train of thought, for to me garrison life offered few attractions. I tried to picture my future chief, Captain Mironoff. I imagined a severe, morose old man, knowing nothing outside of the service, ready to arrest me for the least slip. Dusk was falling; we were advancing rapidly.

"How far is it from here to the fortress?" said I to the coachman.

"You can see it now," he answered.

I looked on all sides, expecting to see high bastions, a wall, and a ditch. I saw nothing but a little village surrounded by a wooden palisade. On one side stood some hay-stacks half covered with snow; on the other a wind-mill, leaning to one side; the wings of the mill, made of the heavy bark of the linden tree, hung idle.

"Where is the fortress?" I asked, astonished.

"There it is," said the coachman, pointing to the village which we had just entered. I saw near the gate an old iron cannon. The streets were narrow and winding, and nearly all the huts were thatched with straw. I ordered the coachman to drive to the Commandant's, and almost immediately my kibitka stopped before a wooden house built on an eminence near the church, which was also of wood. From the front door I entered the waiting-room. An old pensioner, seated on a table, was sewing a blue piece on the elbow of a green uniform. I told him to announce me.

"Enter, my good sir," said he, "our people are at home."

I entered a very neat room, furnished in the fashion of other days. On one side stood a cabinet containing the silver. Against the wall hung the diploma of an officer, with colored engravings arranged around its frame; notably, the "Choice of the Betrothed," the "Taking of Kurstrin," and the "Burial of the Cat by the Mice." Near the window sat an old woman in a mantilla, her head wrapped in a handkerchief. She was winding a skein of thread held on the separated hands of a little old man, blind of one eye, who was dressed like an officer.

"What do you desire, my dear sir?" said the woman to me, without interrupting her occupation. I told her that I had come to enter the service, and that, according to rule, I hastened to present myself to the captain. In saying this, I turned to the one-eyed old man, whom I took for the commandant. The good lady interrupted the speech which I had prepared in advance:

"Ivan Mironoff is not at home; he is gone to visit Father

Alexander Pushkin

Garasim; but it is all the same; I am his wife. Deign to love us and have us in favor! Take a seat, my dear sir." She ordered a servant to send her the Corporal. The little old man gazed at me curiously, with his only eye.

"May I dare to ask," said he, "in what regiment you have deigned to serve?"

I satisfied him on that point.

"And may I dare to ask why you changed from the Guards to our garrison?"

I replied that it was by the orders of authority.

"Probably for actions little becoming an officer of the Guards?" resumed the persistent questioner.

"Will you stop your stupidities?" said the Captain's wife to him. "You see the young man is fatigued by the journey; he has something else to do besides answering you. Hold your hands better! And you my dear sir," continued she, turning to me, "do not be too much afflicted that you are thrust into our little town; you are not the first, and will not be the last. Now, there is Alexis Chabrine, who has been transferred to us for a term of four years for murder. God knows what provocation he had. He and a lieutenant went outside the city with their swords, and before two witnesses Alexis killed the lieutenant. Ah! misfortune has no master."

Just then the Corporal entered, a young and handsome Cossack. "Maxim," said the Captain's wife, "give this officer a clean lodging."

"I obey, Basilia," replied the Cossack; "shall I lodge him

with Ivan Pologoff?"

"You are doting, Maxim, he has too little space now; besides, he is my child's godfather; and, moreover, he never forgets that we are his chiefs. What is your name, my dear sir?"

"Peter Grineff."

"Then conduct Peter Grineff to the quarters of Simeon Kieff. That rascal let his horse into my vegetable garden. Is all right, Maxim?"

"Thank God, all is quiet, except that Corporal Kourzoff quarreled with the woman Augustina about a pail of warm water."

"Ignatius," said the Captain's wife to the one-eyed man, "judge between the two—decide which one is guilty, and punish both. Go, Maxim, God be with you. Peter Grineff, Maxim will conduct you to your lodgings."

I took my leave; the Corporal led me to a cabin placed on the high bank near the river's edge, at the end of the fortress. Half of the cabin was occupied by the family of Simeon Kieff, the other was given up to me. My half of the cabin was a large apartment divided by a partition. Saveliitch began at once to install us, whilst I looked out of the narrow window. Before me stretched the bleak and barren steppe; nearer rose some cabins; at the threshold of one stood a woman with a bowl in her hand calling the pigs to feed; no other objects met my sight, save a few chickens scratching for stray kernels of corn in the street. And this was the country to which I was condemned to pass my youth! I turned from the window, seized by bitter sadness, and went to bed without supper, notwithstanding the supplications of Saveliitch, who with anguish cried aloud: "Oh! he will not deign to eat! O Lord! what will my mistress say, if the child should fall ill!"

The next morning I had scarcely begun to dress, when a young officer entered my room. He was of small size, with irregular features, but his sun-burned face had remarkable vivacity. "Pardon me," said he in French, "that I come so unceremoniously to make your acquaintance. I learned yesterday of your arrival, and the desire of seeing at last a human face so took possession of me that I could wait no longer. You will understand this when you shall have lived here some time!"

I easily guessed that he was the officer dismissed from the Guards for the affair of the duel—Alexis Chabrine. He was very intelligent; his conversation was sprightly and interesting. He described with impulse and gayety the Commandant's family, society, and in general the whole country round. I was laughing heartily, when Ignatius, the same old pensioner whom I had seen mending his uniform in the Captain's waiting- room, entered, and gave me an invitation to dinner from Basilia Mironoff, the Captain's wife. Alexis declared that he would accompany me.

Approaching the Commandant's house we saw on the square some twenty little old pensioners, with long que-ues and three-cornered hats. These old men were drawn up in line of battle. Before them stood the Commandant, a fresh and vigorous old man of high stature, in dressing-gown and cotton cap. As soon as he saw us, he approached, addressed me a few affable words, and then resumed his drill. We were going to stay to see the manoeuvering, but he begged us to go on immediately to the house, promising to join us at once; "for," said he, "there is really nothing to be seen here."

Basilia received us kindly, and with simplicity, treating me like an old acquaintance. The pensioner and the maid Polacca were laying the table-cloth.

"What is the matter with my dear Ivan Mironoff, today, that he is so long instructing his troops?" said the mistress. "Polacca, go and bring him to dinner. And where is my child, Marie?" Scarcely had she pronounced this name, than a young girl about sixteen entered the room;—a rosy, round-faced girl, wearing her hair in smooth bandeaux caught behind her ears, which were red with modesty and shyness. She did not please me very much at the first glance; I was prejudiced against her by Alexis, who had described the Captain's daughter to me as a fool. Marie seated herself in a corner and began to sew. The soup was brought on the table. Basilia, not seeing her husband coming, sent the maid a second time to call him.

"Tell the master that his inspection can wait; the soup is cooling. Thank God! the drills need not be lost; there will be time enough yet to use his voice at his leisure."

The captain soon appeared with his one-eyed officer.

"What's this, my dear," said Basilia; "the table has been served some time, and no one could make you come."

"You see, Basilia, I was busy with the service, instructing my good soldiers."

"Come, come, Ivan Mironoff, that's boasting. The service does not suit them, and as for you, you know nothing about it. You should have stayed at home and prayed God, that suits you much better. My dear guests, to table."

We took our places for dinner. Basilia was not silent a moment; she overwhelmed me with questions: Who were my parents? Were they living? Where did they reside? What was their fortune? When she learned that my father owned three hundred serfs, she exclaimed:

"You see there are some rich people in the world—and we, my dear sir, in point of souls, we possess only the maid Polacca. Yet, thank God, we live, somehow or other. We have but one care, that is Marie, a girl that must be married off. And what fortune has she? The price of two baths per annum. If only she could find a worthy husband. If not, there she is, eternally a maid."

I glanced at Marie; she blushed, tears were dropping into her soup. I pitied her, and hastened to change the conversation. "I have heard that the Bashkirs intend to attack your fortress?"

"Who said so," replied Ivan Mironoff.

"I heard it at Orenbourg."

"All nonsense," said Ivan, "we have not heard the least word about it; the Bashkirs are an intimidated people; and the Kirghis have also had some good lessons. They dare not attack us, and if they should even dream of it, I would give them so great a fright that they would not move again for ten years."

"Do you not fear," I continued, addressing Basilia, "to stay in a fortress exposed to these dangers?"

"A matter of habit, my dear," she replied, "twenty years ago, when we were transferred here from the regiment, you could not believe how I feared the pagans. If I chanced to see their fur caps, if I heard their shouts, believe me, my heart was ready to faint; but now I am so used to this life, that if told that the brigands were prowling around us, I would not stir from the fortress."

"Basilia is a very brave lady," observed Alexis, gravely. "Ivan Mironoff knows some thing about it."

"Oh, you see," said Ivan, "she does not belong to the regiment of poltroons."

"And Marie," I asked of her mother "is she as bold as you?"

"Marie?" said the lady. "No! Marie is a coward. Up to the present she has not heard the report of a gun without trembling in every limb. Two years ago Ivan had a pleasant fancy to fire off his cannon on my birthday; the poor pigeon was so frightened that she almost went into the next world. Since that day the miserable cannon has not spoken."

We rose from the table. The captain and his wife went to take their siesta. I went with Alexis to his room, where we passed the evening together.

IV

THE DUEL

Several weeks elapsed, during which my life in the fortress became not only supportable, but even agreeable. I was received as a member of the family in the Commandant's house. The husband and wife were excellent people. Ivan Mironoff, from being the adopted child of the regiment, rose to officer's rank. He was a plain, simple, uneducated man, but thoroughly good and loyal. His wife governed him, and that suited his natural indolence. Basilia directed the affairs of the garrison, as she did her household, and commanded through the fortress as she did in her own kitchen. Marie soon lost her shyness, and as we became better acquainted I found that she was a girl full of affection and intelligence. Little by little I became deeply attached to this good family.

I was promoted, and ranked as an officer. Military service did not oppress me. In this fortress, blessed by God, there was no duty to do, no guard to mount, nor review to pass. Occasionally, for his own amusement, the Commandant drilled his soldiers. He had not yet succeeded in teaching them which was the right flank and which the left.

Alexis had some French books, and in my idleness I set

work to read, so that a taste for literature awoke within me. I read every morning, and essayed some translations, even metrical compositions. Almost every day I dined at the Commandant's, where, as a general thing, I spent the rest of the day. In the evening, Father Garasim came with his wife, Accoulina, the greatest gossip of the place. Of course Alexis and I met daily, yet gradually his society displeased me. His perpetual jokes upon the Commandant's family, and above all his biting remarks about Marie, rendered his conversation very disagreeable to me. I had no other society than this family in the fortress, and I desired no other. All predictions to the contrary, the Bashkirs did not revolt, and peace reigned around us.

I have already said that I busied myself somewhat with literature. One day I happened to write a little song, of which I was proud. It is well known that authors, under pretext of asking advice, willingly seek a kindly audience. I copied my little song and took it to Alexis, the only one in the fortress who could appreciate a poetical work. After preluding a little, I drew my pages from my pocket and read my verses to him.

"How do you like that?" said I, expecting praise as a tribute due me. To my great annoyance, Alexis, who was generally pleased with my writings, declared frankly that my song was worth nothing.

"What do you mean?" said I, with forced calmness. He took the paper out of my hand and began to criticize without pity, every verse, every word, tearing me up in the most malicious fashion. It was too much. I snatched the paper from him, declaring that never again would I show him any of my compositions.

"We shall see," said he, "if you can keep your word; poets

need a listener as Ivan Mironoff needs a decanter of brandy before dinner. Who is this Marie to whom you declare your tender feelings? Might it not be Marie Mironoff?"

"That is none of your business," said I, frowning. "I want neither your advice nor supposition."

"Oh! oh! vain poet; discreet lover," continued Alexis, irritating me more and more, "listen to friendly counsel: if you want to succeed do not confine yourself to songs."

"What do you mean, sir? Explain!"

"With pleasure," he replied. "I mean that if you wish to form an intimacy with Marie Mironoff, you have only to give her a pair of earrings instead of your lackadaisical verses."

All my blood boiled. "Why have you this opinion of her?" I asked, with much effort restraining my anger.

"Because," said he, "of my own experience."

"You lie, wretch," I cried, with furry, "you lie, shame-lessly."

Alexis was enraged.

"That shall not pass so," he said, grasping my hand. "You shall give me satisfaction."

"When ever you like," I replied, joyfully, for at that moment I was ready to tear him to pieces. I ran at once to see Ivan Ignatius, whom I found with a needle in his hand. According to orders from the Commandant's wife, he was stringing mushrooms which were to be dried for winter use.

"Ah! Peter Grineff, be welcome. Dare I ask on what business God sends you here?"

In a few words I told him of my quarrel with Alexis, and begged him, Ignatius, to be my second. Ignatius heard me to the end with great attention, opening wide his only eye.

"You deign to say that you want to kill Alexis, and desire that I should witness the act? Is that what you mean, dare I ask?"

"Precisely."

"Ah! what folly; you have had some words with Alexis. What then? A harsh word can not be hung up by the neck. He gives you impertinence, give him the same; if he give you a slap, return the blow; he a second, you a third; in the end we will compel you to make peace. Whilst if you fight—well, if *you* should kill *him*, God be with him! for I do not like him much; but if he should perforate you, what a nice piece of business! Then who will pay for the broken pots?"

The arguments of the prudent officer did not shake my resolution.

"Do as you like," said Ignatius, "but what's the use of having me as a witness? People fight—that's nothing extraordinary—I have often been quite close to Swedes and Turks, and people of all shades of color."

I tried to explain to him the duties of a second; Ignatius would not, or could not understand me. "Follow your own

Alexander Pushkin

fashion," said he, "if I were to meddle in this affair, it would be to announce to Ivan Mironoff, according to rule, that a plot is being made in the fortress for the commission of a criminal action—one contrary to the interests of the crown."

I was alarmed, and begged Ignatius to say nothing to the Commandant. He gave me his word that he would be silent, and I left him in peace. As usual I passed the evening at the Commandant's, forcing myself to be calm and gay, in order not to awaken suspicions and to avoid questioning. I confess that I had not the coolness of which people boast who have been in a similar position. I was disposed to tenderness. Marie Mironoff seemed more attractive than ever. The idea that perhaps I saw her for the last time, gave her a touching grace.

Alexis entered. I took him aside and told him of my conversation with Ignatius.

"What's the good of seconds," said he, dryly. "We can do without them."

We agreed to fight behind the haystack the next morning at six o'clock.

Seeing us talking amicably, Ignatius, full of joy, nearly betrayed us. "You should have done that long ago, for a bad peace is better than a good quarrel."

"What! what! Ignatius," said the Captain's wife, who was playing patience in a corner, "I do not quite understand?"

Ignatius, seeing my displeasure, remembered his promise, became confused and knew not what to answer. Alexis came to his relief: "He approves of peace."

"With whom had you quarreled?" said she.

"With Peter Grineff—a few high words."

"Why?"

"For a mere nothing—a song."

"Fine cause for a quarrel! a song! Tell me how it happened."

"Willingly: Peter has recently been composing, and this morning he sang his song for me. Then I chanted mine:

'Daughter of the Captain, walk not forth at midnight.'

As we were not on the same note, Peter was angry, forgetting that every one is at liberty to sing what he pleases."

The insolence of Alexis made me furious. No one but myself understood his allusions. From poetry the conversation passed to poets in general. The Commandant observed that they were all debauchees and drunkards, and advised me, as a friend, to renounce poetry as contrary to the service, and leading to nothing good.

As the pretence of Alexis was to me insupportable, I hastened to take leave of the family. In my own apartment I examined my sword, tried its point, and went to bed, having ordered Saveliitch to wake me in the morning at six o'clock.

The next day at the appointed time I was behind the haystack awaiting my adversary, who did not fail to appear. "We may be surprised," he said; "be quick." We laid aside our uniforms, drew our swords from the scabbards, when Ignatius, followed by five pensioners, came out from behind a haystack. He ordered us to repair to the presence of the Commandant. We obeyed. The soldiers surrounded us. Ignatius conducted us in triumph, marching military step, with majestic gravity. We entered the Commandant's house; Ignatius opened the folding doors, and exclaimed with emphasis: "They are taken!"

Basilia ran toward us: "What does this mean? plotting an assassination in our fortress! Ivan Mironoff, arrest them! Peter Grineff, Alexis, give up your swords to the garret. Peter, I did not expect this of you; are you not ashamed? As for Alexis, it is quite different; he was transferred to us from the Guards for having caused a soul to perish; and he does not believe in our blessed Saviour."

Ivan Mironoff approved increasingly all that his wife said: "You see! You see! Basilia is right, duels are forbidden by the military code."

Meantime Polacca had carried off our swords to the garret. I could not help smiling at this scene. Alexis preserved all his gravity, and said to Basilia: "Notwithstanding all my respect for you, I must say you take useless pains to subject us to your tribunal. Leave that duty to Ivan Mironoff; it is his business."

"What! what! my dear sir," said the lady, "are not man and wife the same flesh and spirit? Ivan Mironoff, are you trifling? Lock up these boys instantly; put them in separate rooms—on bread and water, to expel this stupid idea of theirs. Let Father Garasim give them a penance on order that they may repent before God and man."

Ivan Mironoff did not know what to do. Marie was

extremely pale. The tempest, however, subsided little by little. Basilia ordered us to embrace each other, and the maid was sent for our swords. We left the house, having in appearance made friends. Ignatius re-conducted us.

"Are you not ashamed of yourself," I said to him, "to have denounced us to the Commandant, after having given me your word you would not do so?"

"As God is holy, I said nothing to Ivan Mironoff. Basilia drew it all from me. She took all the necessary measures without the knowledge of the Commandant. Thank God it finished as it did." He went to his room; I remained with Alexis.

"Our affair can not end thus," I remarked.

"Certainly not," replied Alexis. "You shall pay me with your blood for your impertinence, but as undoubtedly we shall be watched, let us feign for a few days. Until then, adieu!"

We separated as if nothing had happened. I returned to the Commandant's, and seated myself as usual near Marie. Her father was absent and her mother busy with house-hold duties. We spoke in subdued tones. Marie reproached me gently for the pain my quarrel with Alexis gave her. "My heart failed me," she said, "when I heard you were going to fight with swords. How strange men are! For a word, they are ready to strangle each other, and sacrifice, not only their own life, but even the honor and happiness of those who—I am sure you did not begin the quarrel? Alexis was the aggressor?"

"Why do you think so?"

Alexander Pushkin

"Because he is so sarcastic. I do not like him, and yet I would not displease him, although he is quite disagreeable to me."

"What do you think, Marie, are you pleasing to him or not?"

Marie blushed. "It seems," said she, "that I please him."

"How do you know?"

"Because he made me an offer of marriage."

"He made you an offer of marriage! When?"

"Last year, two months before your arrival."

"You did not accept?"

"Evidently not, as you see. Alexis is a most intelligent man, of an excellent family and not without fortune, but the mere idea that beneath the crown, on my marriage day, I should be obliged to kiss him before every one! No! no! not for any thing in the world."

Marie's words opened my eyes. I understood the persistence of Alexis in aspersing her character. He had probably remarked our mutual inclination, and was trying to turn us from each other. The words which had provoked our quarrel seemed to me the more infamous, as instead of being a vulgar joke, it was deliberate calumny. The desire to punish this shameless liar became so strong that I waited impatiently the favorable moment. I had not long to wait. The next day, occupied composing an elegy, biting my pen in the expectation of a rhyme, Alexis knocked at my window. I put down my pen, took my sword, and went out of the house.

"Why defer?" said Alexis, "we are no longer watched, let us go down to the river-side; there none will hinder us."

We set out in silence, and having descended a steep path, we stopped at the water's edge and crossed swords. Alexis was more skillful than I in the use of arms, but I was stronger and bolder. Mons. Beaupre, who had been, amongst other things, a soldier, had taught me fencing. Alexis did not expect to find in me an adversary of so dangerous a character.

For some minutes neither gained any advantage over the other, but at last noticing that Alexis was growing weak, I attacked him energetically, and almost drove him backward into the river, when suddenly I heard my name pronounced in a high voice. Turning my head rapidly, I saw Saveliitch running toward me down the path. As I turned my head, I felt a sharp thrust in the breast under the right shoulder, and I fell, unconscious.

V

LOVE

When I came to myself, I neither knew what had happened nor where I was. I felt very weak; the room was strange, there was Saveliitch standing before me, a light in his hand, and some one arranging the bandages that bound my chest and shoulder. Gradually I recalled my duel, and easily divined that I had been wounded. The door at this instant moaned gently on its hinges.

"Well, how is he?" whispered a voice that made me start.

"Still in the same state," sighed Saveliitch, "now unconscious four days." I wanted to turn on my bed, but I had not the strength. "Where am I?" said I, with effort, "who is here?" Marie approached, and bending over me said, gently, "How do you feel?"

"Thank God, I am well. Is that Marie? tell me—?" I could not finish. Saveliitch uttered a cry of joy, his delight showing plainly in his face. "He recovers! he recovers! Thanks to thee, O God! Peter, how you frightened me!— four days! It is easy to talk—!"

Marie interrupted him: "Do not, Saveliitch, speak too

much to him; he is still very weak." She went out, shutting the door noiselessly. I must be in the Commandant's house, or Marie could not come to see me. I wished to question Saveliitch, but the old man shook his head and put his fingers in his ears. I closed my eyes from ill-humor—and fell asleep.

Upon awaking, I called Saveliitch; instead of him, I saw before me Marie, whose gentle voice greeted me. I seized her hand and bathed it with my tears. Marie did not withdraw it, and suddenly I felt upon my cheek the impression, humid and delicious, of her lips! A thrill shot through my whole being.

"Dear, good Marie, be my wife, and make me the happiest of men!"

"In the name of heaven be calm," she said, withdrawing her hand, "your wound may reopen; for my sake be careful."

She left the room. I was in a daze. I felt life returning. "She will be mine!" I kept repeating, "she loves me!" I grew better, hour by hour. The barber of the regiment dressed my wounds, for there was no other physician in the fortress, and thank God, he did not merely play the doctor. Youth and nature completed the cure.

The Commandant's whole family surrounded me with care. Marie scarcely ever left me. I need not say that I took the first favorable moment to continue my interrupted declaration. This time Marie listened with more patience. She frankly acknowledged her affection for me. And added that her parents would be happy in her happiness; "but," she continued, "think well of it? Will there be no objection on the part of your family?"

Alexander Pushkin

I did not doubt my mother's tenderness, but knowing my father's character, I foresaw that my love would not be received by him favorably, and that in all probability he would treat it as one of my youthful follies. This I avowed plainly to Marie, but nevertheless I resolved to write to my father as eloquently as possible, and ask his blessing on our marriage. I showed the letter to Marie, who thought it so touching and convincing that she did not doubt of success, and abandoned herself, with all the confidence of youth and love, to the feelings of her heart.

I made peace with Alexis in the first days of my convalescence. Ivan Mironoff said, reproaching me for the duel: "You see, Peter, I ought to put you under arrest, but indeed you have been well punished without that. Alexis is, by my orders, under guard in the barn, and his sword is under lock and key in Basilia's keeping."

I was too happy to harbor spite, so I entreated for Alexis, and the kind Commandant, with his wife's permission, consented to set him at liberty. Alexis came at once to see me. He expressed regret for all that had happened, confessing that the fault was all his, and begged me to forget the past. Being naturally incapable of revenge, I pardoned him, forgiving both our quarrel and my wound. In his calumny I now saw the irritation of wounded vanity and despised love. I generously forgave my unfortunate rival. As soon as completely cured I returned to my lodging. I awaited impatiently the reply to my letter, not daring to hope, yet trying to stifle all sad presentiments. I had not yet had an explanation with Basilia and her husband, but my suit could not surprise them. Neither Marie nor I had concealed our feelings, and we were sure in advance of their consent.

At last, one pleasant day Saveliitch came to my room,

letter in hand. The address was written in my father's hand. This sight prepared me for something grave, for usually my mother wrote me, and he only added a few lines at the end. Long I hesitated to break the seal. I read again and again the solemn superscription:

"To my Son,
Peter Grineff,
Principality of Orenbourg,
Fortress of Belogorsk."

I tried to discover by my father's writing his mood of mind when he wrote that letter. At last I broke that seal. I saw from the first lines that our hopes were crushed! Here is the letter:

"MY SON PETER: We received the 15th of this month the letter in which you ask our paternal benediction and consent to your marriage with Mironoff's daughter. Not only have I no intention of giving either my consent or benediction, but I have a great mind to go to you and punish you for your childish follies, notwithstanding your officer's rank, because you have proved that you are not worthy to bear the sword which was given you for the defense of your country, and not for the purpose of fighting a duel with a fool of your own stamp. I shall write instantly to Andrew Karlovitch to transfer you from the fortress of Belogorsk to some still more distant place. Upon hearing of your wound your mother was taken ill, and is still confined to her bed. What will become of you? I pray God to reform you, but can scarcely hope for so much from his goodness. Your father,

A.G."

The harsh expressions which my father had not spared, wounded me sorely; the contempt with which he treated Marie seemed to me as unjust as it was undignified. Then the mere idea of being sent from this fortress alarmed me; but above all, I grieved for my mother's illness. Saveliitch came in for a share of my indignation, not doubting but that he informed my parents of the duel. After having paced up and down my little chamber, I stopped suddenly before the old man and said: "It seems that it is not enough that you caused my wound, and brought me almost to the brink of the grave, but that you want to kill my mother too!"

Saveliitch was as motionless as if lightning had struck him. "Have mercy on me! my lord," said he, "what do you deign to tell me? I caused your wound? God sees that I was running to put my breast before you, to receive the sword of Alexis. This cursed age of mine hindered me. But what have I done to your mother?"

"What have you done? Who charged you to write an accusation against me? Were you taken into my service to play the spy on me?"

"I write an accusation?" replied the old man, quite broken down, "O God! King of heaven! Here, read what the master writes me, and you shall see if I denounced thee." At the same time he drew from his pocket a letter which he gave me, and I read what follows:

"Shame upon you, you old dog, that notwithstanding my strict orders you wrote me nothing regarding my son, leaving to strangers the duty of telling me of his follies. Is it thus you do your duty and fulfill your master's will? I shall send you to keep the pigs, for having concealed the truth, and for your condescension to the young man. Upon receipt of this letter inform me immediately of the state of his health, which is, I hear, improving, and tell me precisely the place of his wound, and whether he has well attended."

Evidently Saveliitch was not in the wrong, and I had offended him by my suspicions and reproaches. I asked him to forgive me, but the old man was inconsolable. "See to what I have lived!" he repeated; "see what thanks I have merited from my masters for all my long services! I am an old dog! I am a swine-herd, and more than all that, I caused your wound. No, no, Peter, I am not in fault, it is the cursed Frenchman who taught thee to play with these steel blades, and to stamp and dance, as if by thrusting and dancing you could defend yourself from a bad man."

Now, then, who had taken the pains to accuse me to my father? The General, Andrew Karlovitch? He did not trouble himself much about me; moreover, Ivan Mironoff had not thought it worth while to report my duel to him. My suspicions fell on Alexis. He only would find some advantage in this information, the consequence of which might be my dismissal from the fortress and separation from the Commandant's family. I went to tell every thing to Marie. She met me on the doorstep.

"What has happened to you? how pale you are!"

"All's over," I replied, handing her my father's letter.

It was her turn to blanch. Having read the letter she returned it, and said in a trembling voice: "It was not my destiny. Your parents do not wish me in their family; may the will of God be done! He knows better than we what is best for us. There is nothing to be done in the matter,

Peter; you, at least, may be happy."

"It shall not be so," I exclaimed, taking her hand. "You love me, I am ready for any fate. Let us go and throw ourselves at your parents' feet. They are simple people; they are neither haughty nor cruel; they will give us their benediction; we will marry; and in time, I am sure, we will soften my father. My mother will intercede for us, and he will pardon me."

"No, Peter, I will not marry you without the benediction of your parents. You would not be happy without their blessing. Let us submit to the will of God. If you meet another bride, if you love her, may God be with you! I, Peter, I will pray for both of you." Tears interrupted her, and she went away; I wished to follow her into the house, but I was not master of myself, and I went to my own quarters. I was plunged in melancholy, when Saveliitch came to interrupt my reflections.

"There, my lord," said he, presenting me a sheet of paper all covered with writing, "see if I am a spy on my master, and if I try to embroil father and son."

I took the paper from his hand; it was his reply to my father's letter.

I could not help smiling at the old man's letter. I was in no condition to write to my father, and to calm my mother his letter seemed sufficient.

From that day, Marie scarcely spoke to me, and even tried to avoid me. The Commandant's house became insupportable, and I accustomed myself, little by little, to remain alone in my room. At first Basilia reasoned with me, but seeing my persistency she let me alone. I saw Ivan

Mironoff only when the service required it. I had but rare interviews with Alexis, for whom my antipathy increased, because I thought I discovered in him a secret enmity which confirmed my suspicions. Life became a burden; I gave myself up to a melancholy which was fed by solitude and inaction. Love burned on in silence and tortured me, more and more. I lost all taste for reading and literature; I let myself become completely depressed; and I feared that I should either become a lunatic or rush into dissipation, when events occurred that had great influence on my life and give a strong and healthy tone to my mind.

Alexander Pushkin

VI

POUGATCHEFF

Before beginning the recital of the strange events of which I was witness, I ought to say a few words about the situation of affairs toward the end of the year 1773. The rich and vast province of Orenbourg was inhabited by a number of tribes, half civilized, who had just recognized the sovereignty of the Russian Czars. Their continual revolts, their impatience of law and civilized life, their inconstancy and cruelty, demanded on the part of the government a constant watchfulness to reduce them to obedience. Fortresses had been erected in favorable places, and Cossacks, the former possessors of the shores of the Iaik, in many places formed a part of the garrisons. But these very Cossacks, who should have guaranteed the peace and security of their districts, were restless and dangerous subjects of the empire. In 1772 a riot occurred in one of their chief towns. This riot was caused by the severity of the measures employed by General Trauben-berg to bring the army to obedience. The only result of these measures was the barbarous murder of Traubenberg, a change of Imperial officers, and in the end, by force of grape and canister, the suppression of the riot.

This happened shortly before my arrival at the fortress of

Belogorsk. Then all seemed quiet. But the authorities had too easily believed in the feigned repentance of the rebels, who nursed their hate in silence, and only awaited a propitious moment to recommence the struggle.

I return to my story. Once evening, it was in the month of October, 1773, I was alone in the house, listening to the whistling of the Autumn winds, and watching the clouds gliding rapidly before the moon. An order came from the Commandant, calling me to his presence. I went that instant. I found there Alexis, Ignatius and the Corporal of the Cossacks, but neither the wife nor daughter of the Commandant. My chief bade me good evening, had the door closed, and every one seated, except the Corporal who remained standing; then he drew a paper from his pocket and said to us:

"Gentlemen, important news! Listen to what the General writes." He put on his spectacles and read:

"To the Commandant of the Fortress of Belogorsk, Captain Mironoff. *Confidential*. I hereby inform you that the deserter and turbulent Cossack of the Don, Imiliane Pougatcheff, after having been guilty of the unpardonable insolence of usurping the name of the deceased Emperor Peter III, has assembled a troop of brigands, disturbed the villages of the Iaik, and has even taken and destroyed several fortresses, at the same time committing everywhere robberies and assassinations. Therefore, upon the receipt of this, you will, Captain, bethink you of the measures to be taken to repulse the said robber and usurper; and if possible, in case he turn his arms against the fortress confided to your care, to completely exterminate him."

"It is easy to talk," said the Commandant, taking off his

spectacles, and folding the paper; "but we must use every precaution. The rascal seems strong, and we have only 130 men, even adding the Cossacks, upon whom there is no dependence, be it said without reproach to thee, Maxim." The Corporal of the Cossacks smiled. "Gentlemen, let us do our part; be vigilant, post sentries, establish night patrols; in case of an attack, shut the gates and call out the soldiers. Maxim, watch well your Cossacks. It is necessary to examine the cannon and clean it; and above all to keep the secret, that no one in the fortress should know any thing before the time."

Having given his orders, Ivan Mironoff dismissed us. I went out with Alexis, speculating on what we had heard. "What do you think of it? How will this end?" I asked him.

"God knows," he replied, "we shall see. At present there is no danger." And he began, as if thinking, to hum a French air.

Notwithstanding our precautions the news of the apparition of Pougatcheff spread through the fortress. However great the respect of Ivan Mironoff for his wife, he would not reveal to her for anything in the world a military secret. When he had received the General's letter he very adroitly rid himself of Basilia by telling her that the Greek priest had received from Orenbourg extraordinary news which he kept a great mystery. Thereupon Basilia desired to pay a visit to Accouline, the clergyman's wife, and by Mironoff's advice Marie went also. Master of the situation, Ivan Mironoff locked up the maid in the kitchen and assembled us.

Basilia came home without news, and learned that during her absence a council of war had been held, and that

Polacca was imprisoned in the kitchen. She suspected that her husband had deceived her, and overwhelmed him with questions. He was prepared for the attack, and stoutly replied to his curious better-half:

"You see, my dear, the women about the country have been using straw to kindle their fires; now as that might be dangerous, I assembled my officers, and gave them orders to prevent these women lighting fires with anything but fagots and brushwood."

"And why did you lock up Polacca in the kitchen till my return?" Ivan Mironoff had not foreseen that question, and muttered some incoherent words. Basilia saw at once her husband's perfidy, but knowing that she could extract nothing from him at that moment, she ceased her questioning, and spoke of the pickled cucumbers which Accouline knew how to prepare in a superior fashion. That night Basilia never closed an eye, unable to imagine what it was that her husband knew that she could not share with him.

The next day, returning from mass, she saw Ignatius cleaning the cannon, taking out rags, pebbles, bits of wood, and all sorts of rubbish which the small boys had stuffed there. "What means these warlike preparations?" thought the Commandant's wife? "Is an attack from the Kirghis feared? Is it possible that Mironoff would hide from me so mere a trifle?" She called Ignatius, determined to know the secret that excited her woman's curiosity. Basilia began by making some remarks about household matters, like a judge who begins his interrogation with questions foreign to the affair, in order to reassure the accused, and throw him off his guard. Then having paused a moment she sighed and shook her head, saying: "O God! what news! what news! What will become of us?"

Alexander Pushkin

"My dear lady," said Ignatius, "the Lord is merciful; we have soldiers and plenty of powder; I have cleaned the cannon. We may repulse this Pougatcheff. If the Lord is with us, the wolf will eat no one here."

"Who is Pougatcheff?" asked the Commandant's wife.

Ignatius saw that he had gone too far, and he bit his tongue. But it was too late. Basilia constrained him to tell her all, having given her word to keep the secret. She kept her word, and indeed told no one except Accoulina, whose cow was still on the steppe and might be carried off by the brigands. Soon every one talked of Pougatcheff, the current reports being very different. The Commandant sent out the Corporal to pick up information about him in all the neighboring villages and little forts. The Corporal returned after an absence of two days, and declared that he had seen on the steppe, sixty versts from the fortress, a great many fires, and that he had heard the Bashkirs say that an innumerable force was advancing. He could not tell anything definitely, having been afraid to venture farther.

Great agitation was soon after this observed amongst the Cossacks of our garrison. They assembled in groups in the streets, speaking in a low tone amongst themselves, and dispersing as soon as they perceived a dragoon or other Russian soldier. Orders were given to watch them. Zoulac, a baptized Kalmouk, made a very grave revelation to the Commandant. According to the Kalmouk, the Cossack made a false report; for to his comrades the perfidious Corporal said that he had advanced to the rebel camp, had been presented to their rebel chief, had kissed his hand and conversed with him. The Commandant ordered the Corporal under arrest, and replaced him by the Kalmouk. This change was received by the Cossacks with visible discontent. They openly murmured and Ignatius, when executing the Commandant's order, heard them say, with his own ears, "wait, garrison rat, wait!"

The Commandant decided to examine the Corporal that same day, but he had escaped, no doubt, by the aid of his brother Cossacks. Another event increased the Captain's uneasiness. A Bashkir was seized bearing seditious letters. Upon this occasion, the Commandant decided to call at once a council, and in order to do so, wished to send away his wife under some specious pretext. But as Mironoff was the simplest and most truthful of men, he could think of no other device than that already employed.

"You see, Basilia," said he, coughing several times, "Father Garasim has, it is said, been to the city—"

"Silence! silence!" interrupted his wife; "you are going to call another council and talk in my absence of Imiliane Pougatcheff, but this time you can not deceive me."

The Captain stared; "Eh! well! my dear," said he, "since you know all, stay; we may as well speak before you."

"You cannot play the fox," said his wife; "send for the officers."

We assembled again. The Commandant read, before his wife, Pougatcheff's proclamation, written by some half-educated Cossack. The brigand declared to us his intention of marching directly upon our fortress, inviting the Cossacks and soldiers to join him, and advising the chiefs not to resist, threatening, in that case, extremest torture. The proclamation was written in vulgar but energetic terms, and must have produced an impression upon simple-minded people.

Alexander Pushkin

"What a rascal!" exclaimed the Captain's wife. "Just see what he proposes. To go out and meet him and lay our flags at his feet. Ah! the son of a dog! He does not know that we have been forty years in service, and that, thank God, we have seen all sorts of military life. Is it possible to find a Commandant cowardly enough to obey this robber?"

"It ought not to be," replied the Captain, "but it is said that the villain has taken possession of several fortress."

"It appears he is quite strong," said Alexis.

"We shall instantly know his real force," continued the Commandant; "Basilia, give me the key of the garret. Ignatius, bring the Bashkir here, and tell Zoulac to bring the rods."

"Wait a little, my dear," said the Commandant's wife, leaving her seat; "let me take Marie out of the house, or else she will hear the screams and be frightened. And, to tell the truth, I am, myself, not very curious about such investigations. Until I see you again, adieu."

Torture was then so rooted in the customs of justice, that the humane Ukase of Catherine II, who had ordered its abolition, remained long without effect. It was thought that the confession of the accused was indispensable to his condemnation, an idea not only unreasonable, but contrary to the most simple good sense in matters of jurisprudence; for if the denial of the accused is not accepted as proof of his innocence, the confession which is torn from him by torture ought to serve still less as proof of his guilt. Even now I sometimes hear old judges regret the abolition of this barbarous custom. But in the time of our story no one doubted the necessity of torture, neither the judges nor the accused themselves. For this reason the Captain's order did not astonish any of us. Ignatius went for the Bashkir, and a few minutes later he was brought to the waiting-room. The Commandant ordered him into the council-room where we were.

The Bashkir crossed the threshold with difficulty, for his feet were shackled. He took off his high Cossack cap and stood near the door. I looked at him and shuddered, involuntarily. Never shall I forget that man; he seemed at least seventy years of age, and had neither nose nor ears. His head was shaved; a few sparse gray hairs took the place of beard. He was small of stature, thin and bent; but his Tartar eyes still sparkled.

"Eh! eh!" said the Commandant, who recognized by these terrible signs one of the rebels punished in 1741. "You are an old wolf, I see; you have already been caught in our snares. This is not your first offense, for your head is so well planed off."

The old Bashkir was silent, and looked at the Commandant with an air of complete imbecility.

"Well! why are you silent?" continued the Captain; "do you not understand Russian? Zoulac, ask him, in your tongue, who sent him into our fortress."

The Kalmouk repeated in the Tartar language the Captain's question. But the Bashkir looked at him with the same expression and without answering a word.

"I will make you answer," exclaimed the Captain, with a Tartar oath. "Come, take off his striped dressing-gown, his fool's garment, and scourge him well."

Two pensioners commenced to remove the clothing from the shoulders of the old man. Then, sore distress was vividly depicted on the face of the unfortunate man. He looked on all sides, like a poor little animal caught by children. But when one of the pensioners seized his hands to turn them around his neck and lift up the old man on his shoulders; when Zoulac took the rods and raised his hand to strike, then the Bashkir uttered a low, but penetrating moan, and raising his head, opened his mouth, where, in place of a tongue, moved a short stump!

We were still debating, when Basilia rushed breathlessly into the room with a terrified air. "What has happened to you?" asked the Commandant, surprised.

"Misfortune! misfortune!" replied she. "A fort was taken this morning; Father Garasim's boy has just returned. He saw how it was captured. The Commandant and all the officers are hanged, all the soldiers made prisoners, and the rebels are coming here."

This unexpected news made a deep impression on me, for I knew the Commandant of that fortress. Two months ago, the young man, traveling with his bride coming from Orenbourg, had paid a visit to Captain Mironoff. The fort he commanded was only twenty-five versts from ours, so that from hour to hour we might expect an attack from Pougatcheff.

My imagination pictured the fate of Marie, and I trembled for her.

"Listen, Captain Mironoff," said I to the Commandant, "our duty is to defend the fortress to our last breath; that is understood, but the safety of the women must be thought of; send them to a more distant fortress,—to Orenbourg, if the route be still open."

Mironoff turned to his wife. "You see my dear! indeed it would be well to send you somewhere farther off until we shall have defeated the rebels."

"What nonsense!" replied she. "Where is the fortress that balls have not reached? In what respect is our fortress unsafe? Thank God, we have lived here twenty and one years. We have seen Bashkirs and Kirghis; Pougatcheff can not be worse than they."

"My dear, stay if you will, since your faith is so great in our fortress. But what shall we do with Marie? It will be all well if we can keep off the robber, or if help reach us in time. If the fortress, however, be taken—"

Basilia could only stammer a few words, and was silent, choked by her feelings.

"No, Basilia," continued the Commandant, who remarked that his words made a deep impression on his wife, perhaps for the first time in his life, "it is not advisable that Marie stay here. Let us send her to Orenbourg, to her god-mother's. That is a well-manned fortress, with stone walls and plenty of cannon. I would advise you to go there yourself; think what might happen to you were your fortress to be taken by assault."

"Well! well! let us send Marie away," said the Captain's wife, "but do not dream of asking me to go, for I will do nothing of the kind. It is not becoming, in my old age, to separate myself from thee and seek a solitary grave in a strange place. We have lived together; let us die together."

"You are right," said the Commandant. "Go, and equip

Marie; there is no time to lose; tomorrow, at the dawn of day, she shall set out; she must have a convoy, though indeed there is no one to spare. Where is she?"

"She is at Accoulina's," said his wife. "She fainted upon hearing that the fortress had been taken."

Basilia went to prepare for her daughter's departure. The discussion still continued at the Commandant's, but I took no further part in it. Marie reappeared at supper with eyes red from tears. We supped in silence and rose from the table sooner than usual. Having bade the family good night, each one sought his room. I forgot my sword, on purpose, and went back for it; I anticipated finding Marie alone. In truth she met me at the door and gave me my sword.

"Adieu, Peter," she said, weeping, "they send me to Orenbourg. Be happy. Perhaps God will permit us to meet again; if not—"

She burst into tears. I folded her in my arms.

"Adieu, my angel!" I said, "adieu my cherished, my beloved; what ever happens, be sure that my last thought, my last prayer, will be for thee." Leaning of my breast, Marie wept. I kissed her and rushed out.

VII

THE ASSAULT

I could not sleep during the night, and did not even undress. I intended to be at the fortress gates at day-dawn to see Marie set out, and bid her a last adieu. I was completely changed. Excitement was less painful than my former melancholy, for with the grief of separation there mingled vague but secret hope, impatient expectation of danger, and a high ambition. Night passed quickly. I was on the point of going out, when my door opened, and the Corporal entered, saying that our Cossacks had deserted the fortress during the night, forcing with them Zoulac, the Christian Kalmouk, and that all around our ramparts, unknown people were riding. The idea that Marie had not been able to get off, froze me with terror. I gave, in haste, a few instructions to the Corporal, and ran to the Commandant's.

Day was breaking. I was going down the street swiftly when I heard my name called. I stopped.

"Where are you going, dare I ask?" said Ignatius, catching up with me; "the Captain is on the rampart and sends me for you. Pougatcheff is here."

Alexander Pushkin

"Is Marie gone?" I said, shuddering.

"She was not ready in time; communication with Orenbourg is cut off; the fortress is surrounded. Peter, this is bad work."

We went to the rampart—a small height formed by nature and fortified by a palisade. The garrison was there under arms. The cannon had been dragged there the evening before. The Commandant was walking up and down before his little troop—the approach of danger had restored to the old warrior extraordinary vigor. On the steppe, not far from the fortress, there were some twenty horsemen, who looked like Cossacks; but amongst them were a few Bashkirs, easily recognized by their caps and quivers. The Commandant passed before the ranks of his small army and said to the soldiers: "Come, boys, let us fight today for our mother the Empress, and show the world that we are brave men and faithful to our oath."

The soldiers, with loud shouts, testified their good will. Alexis was standing by me examining the enemy. The people on the steppe, seeing, no doubt, some movement in our fort, collected in groups and spoke amongst themselves. The Commandant ordered Ignatius to point the cannon upon them, he himself applying the light. The ball whistled over their heads without doing them any harm. The horsemen dispersed at once, setting off on a gallop, and the steppe became deserted. At this moment Basilia appeared on the rampart, followed by Marie, who would not leave her.

"Well," said the Captain's wife, "how is the battle going? Where is the enemy?"

"The enemy is not far off," replied Ivan, "but if God wills

it, all will be well; and thou, Marie, art thou afraid?"

"No, papa," said Marie, "I am more afraid by myself in the house." She glanced at me, and tried to smile. I pressed my sword, remembering that I had received it from her on the preceding eve, as if for her defense. My heart was on fire. I fancied myself her knight, and longed to prove myself worthy of her trust. I awaited the decisive moment impatiently.

Suddenly coming from behind a hill, eight versts from the fortress, appeared new groups of horsemen, and soon the whole steppe was covered by men armed with lances and arrows. Amongst them, wearing a scarlet cafetan, sword in hand, could be distinguished a man mounted on a white horse. This was Pougatcheff himself. He halted, was surrounded by his followers, and very soon, probably by his orders, four men left the crowd and galloped to our ramparts. We recognized among them our traitors. One of them raised a sheet of paper above his cap and another carried on the point of his lance Zoulac's head, which he threw to us over the palisade. The poor Kalmouk's head rolled at the feet of the Commandant.

The traitors shouted to us: "Do not fire, come out and receive the Czar. The Czar is here."

"Fire!" shouted the Captain as sole reply.

The soldiers discharged their pieces. The Cossack who held the letter, tottered and fell from his horse; the others fled. I glanced at Marie. Petrified by horror at the sight of the Kalmouk's head, dizzy from the noise of the discharge, she seemed lifeless. The Commandant ordered the Corporal to take the letter from the hand of the dead Cossack. Ignatius sallied out and returned, leading by the bridle the man's horse. He gave the letter to Ivan, who read it in a low voice and tore it up. Meantime the rebels were preparing for an attack. Very soon balls whistled about our ears, and arrows fell around us, buried deep in the ground.

"Basilia," said the Captain, "women have nothing to do here; take away Marie; you see the child is more dead than alive." Basilia, whom the sound of the balls had rendered more yielding, glanced at the steppe where much movement was visible, and said: "Ivan, life and death are from God; bless Marie; come, child, to thy father."

Pale and trembling, Marie came and knelt, bending low before him. The old Commandant made three times the sign of the cross over her, then raising, kissed her, and said in a broken voice: "Oh! my dear Marie! pray to God, he will never abandon thee. If an honest man seek thee, may God give you both love and goodness. Live together as we have lived; my wife and I. Adieu! my dear Marie! Basilia, take her away quickly."

Marie put her arms around his neck and sobbed. The Captain's wife, in tears, said: "Embrace us also; adieu, Ivan; if ever I have crossed you, forgive me."

"Adieu! adieu! my dear," said the Commandant, kissing his old companion. "Come! enough! go to the house, and if you have time dress Marie in her best; let her wear a sarafan, embroidered in gold, as is our custom for burial."

Ivan Mironoff returned to us, and fixed all his attention upon the enemy. The rebels collected around their chief and suddenly began to advance. "Be firm, boys," said the Commandant, "the assault begins." At that instant savage war-cries were heard. The rebels were approaching the fortress with their accustomed fleetness. Our cannon was charged with grape and canister. The Commandant let them come within short range, and again put a light to his piece. The shot struck in the midst of the force, which scattered in every direction. Only their chief remained in advance, and he, waving his sabre, seemed to be rallying them. Their piercing shouts, which had ceased an instant, redoubled again. "Now, children," ordered the Captain, "open the gate, beat the drum, and advance! Follow me, for a sortie!"

The Captain, Ignatius and I were in an instant beyond the parapet. But the frightened garrison had not moved from the square. "What are you doing, my children?" shouted the Captain; "if we must die, let us die; the imperial service demands it!"

At this moment the rebels fell upon us, and forced the entrance to the citadel. The drum was silent; the garrison threw down their arms. I had been knocked down, but I rose and entered, pell-mell, with the crowds into the fortress. I saw the Commandant wounded on the head, and closed upon by a small troop of bandits, who demanded the keys. I was running to his aid when several powerful Cossacks seized me and bound me with their long sashes, crying out: "Wait there, traitor to the Czar, till we know what to do with you."

We were dragged along the streets. The inhabitants came out of their houses offering bread and salt. The bells were rung. Suddenly, shouts announced that the Czar was on the square, awaiting to receive the oaths of the prisoners.

Pougatcheff was seated in an arm-chair on the steps of the Commandant's house. He was robed in an elegant Cossack cafetan embroidered on the seams. A high cap of

Alexander Pushkin

martin-skin, ornamented with gold tassels, covered his brow almost to his flashing eyes. His face seemed to me not unknown. Cossack chiefs surrounded him. Father Garasim, pale and trembling, stood, the cross in his hand, at the foot of the steps, and seemed to supplicate in silence for the victims brought before him.

On the square itself, a gallows was hastily erected. When we approached, the Bashkirs opened a passage through the crowd and presented us to Pougatcheff. The bells ceased; the deepest silence prevailed. "Which is the Commandant?" asked the usurper. Our Corporal came out of the crowd and pointed to Mironoff. Pougatcheff looked at the old man with a terrible expression, and said to him: "How did you dare to oppose me, your emperor?"

The Commandant, weakened by his wound, collected all his energy, and said, in a firm but faint voice: "You are not my emperor; you are a usurper and a brigand."

Pougatcheff frowned and raised his white handkerchief. Immediately the old Captain was seized by Cossacks and dragged to the gibbet. Astride the cross-beam of the gallows, sat the mutilated Bashkirs who we had questioned; he held a rope in his hand, and I saw, an instant after, poor Ivan Mironoff suspended in the air. Then Ignatius was brought up before Pougatcheff.

"Take the oath to the emperor, Peter Fedorovitch."

"You are not our emperor," replied the Lieutenant, repeating his Captain's words, "you are a brigand and a usurper."

Pougatcheff again made a signal with his handkerchief, and the kind Ignatius hung beside his ancient chief. It was my turn. I looked boldly at Pougatcheff, preparing to repeat the words of my brave comrades, when to my inexpressible astonishment I saw Alexis amongst the rebels. He had had time to cut his hair round, and exchange his uniform for a Cossack cafetan. He approached Pougatcheff and whispered to him. "Let him be hung," said Pougatcheff, not deigning to look at me. A rope was put around my neck. I uttered a prayer to God in a low voice, expressing sincere repentance for my sins, and imploring him to save all those dear to my heart. I was led beneath the gibbet. A shout was heard, "Stop! Stop!" The executioners paused. I looked. Saveliitch was kneeling at Pougatcheff's feet. "O my lord and master," said my dear old serf, "what do you want with that nobleman's child? Set him free, you will get a good ransom for his life; but for an example, and to frighten the rest, command that I, an old man, shall be hung."

Pougatcheff made a sign. They unbound me at once. "Our emperor pardons you," they said. At the moment I did not know that my deliverance was a cause for joy or for sorrow. My mind was too confused. I was taken again before the usurper and made to kneel at his feet. Pougatcheff offered me his muscular hand. "Kiss his hand! Kiss his hand!" cried out all around me. But I would have preferred the most atrocious torture to a degradation so infamous. "My dear Peter," whispered Saveliitch, who was standing behind me, "do not play the obstinate; what does it cost? Kiss the brigand's hand."

I did not move. Pougatcheff drew back his hand: "His lordship is stupefied with joy; raise him up," said he. I was at liberty. Then I witnessed the continuation of the infamous comedy.

The inhabitants began to take the oath. They went one by

Alexander Pushkin

one to kiss the cross and salute the usurper. After them came the garrison soldiers. The company's tailor, armed with his great blunt-pointed shears, cut off their queues; they shook their heads and kissed the hand of Pougatcheff, who declared them pardoned and received into his troops. This lasted for nearly three hours. At last Pougatcheff rose from his arm-chair and went down the steps, followed by his chiefs. A white horse richly caparisoned was led to him; tow Cossacks helped him into the saddle. He signified to Father Garasim that he would dine with him. At this moment wild heart-rending shrieks from a woman filled the air. Basilia, without her mantle, her hair in disorder, 1was dragged out on the steps; one the brigands had on her mantle; the others were carrying away her chests, her linen, and other household goods. "O good men," she cried, "let me go, take me to Ivan Mironoff." Suddenly she saw the gibbet and recognized her husband. "Wretches," she cried, "What have you done? O my light, Ivan! Brave soldier! no Prussian ball, nor Turkish sabre killed thee, but a vile condemned deserter."

"Silence that old sorceress," said Pougatcheff.

A young Cossack struck her with his sabre on the head. She fell dead at the foot of the steps. Pougatcheff rode off, all the people following.

VIII

THE UNEXPECTED VISIT

I stood in the vacant square, unable to collect my thoughts, disturbed by so many terrible emotions. Uncertainty about Marie's fate tortured me. Where is she? Is she concealed? Is her retreat safe? I went to the Commandant's house. It was in frightful disorder; the chairs, tables, presses had been burned up and the dishes were in fragments. I rushed up the little stairs leading to Marie's room, which I entered for the first time in my life. A lamp still burned before the shrine which had enclosed the sacred objects revered by all true believers. The clothes-press was empty, the bed broke up. The robbers had not taken the little mirror hanging between the door and the window. What had become of the mistress of this simple, virginal abode? A terrible thought flashed through my mind. Marie in hands of the brigands! My heart was torn, and I cried aloud: "Marie! Marie!" I heard a rustle. Polacca, quite pale, came from her hiding-place behind the clothes-press.

"Ah! Peter," said she, clasping her hands, "what a day! what horrors!"

"Marie?" I asked impatiently, "Marie—where is she?"

Alexander Pushkin

"The young lady is alive," said the maid, "concealed at Accoulina's, at the house of the Greek priest."

"Great God!" I cried, with terror, "Pougatcheff is there!"

I rushed out of the room, made a bound into the street and ran wildly to the priest's house. It was ringing with songs, shouts and laughter. Pougatcheff was at table there with his men. Polacca had followed me; I sent her in to call out Accoulina secretly. Accoulina came into the waiting-room, an empty bottle in her hand.

"In the name of heaven, where is Marie?" I asked with agitation.

"The little dove is lying on my bed behind the partition. Oh! Peter, what danger we have just escaped! The rascal had scarcely seated himself at table than the poor thing moaned. I thought I should die of fright. He heard her. 'Who is moaning in your room, old woman?' 'My niece, Czar.' 'Let me see your niece, old woman.' I saluted him humbly; 'My niece, Czar, has not strength to come before your grace.' 'Then I will go and see her.' And will you believe it, he drew the curtains and looked at our dove, with his hawk's eyes! The child did not recognize him. Poor Ivan Mironoff! Basilia! Why was Ignatius taken, and you spared? What do you think of Alexis? He has cut his hair and now hobnobs with them in there. When I spoke of my sick niece he looked at me as if he would run me through with his knife. But he said nothing, and we must be thankful for that."

The drunken shouts of the guests, and the voice of Father Garasim now resounded together; the brigands wanted more wine, and Accoulina was needed. "Go back to your house, Peter," said she, "woe to you, if you fall into his hands!"

She went to serve her guests; I, somewhat quieted, returned to my room. Crossing the square, I saw some Bashkirs stealing the boots from the bodies of the dead. I restrained my useless anger. The brigands had been through the fortress and had pillaged the officers' houses.

I reached my lodging. Saveliitch met me at the threshold. "Thank God!" he cried. "Ah! master, the rascals have taken everything; but what matter, since they did not take your life. Did you not recognize their chief, master?"

"No, I did not; who is he?"

"What, my dear boy, have you forgotten the drunkard who cheated you out of the touloup the day of the snow-drift—a hare-skin touloup?—the rascal burst all the seams putting it on."

My eyes were opened. The resemblance between the guide and Pougatcheff was striking. I now understood the pardon accorded me. I recalled with gratitude the lucky incident. A youth's touloup given to a vagabond had saved my neck; and this drunkard, capturing fortress, had shaken the very empire.

"Will you not deign to eat something?" said Saveliitch, true to his instincts; "there is nothing in the house, it is true, but I will find something and prepare it for you."

Left alone, I began to reflect that not to leave the fortress, now subject to the brigand, or to join his troops, would be unworthy of an officer. Duty required me to go and present myself where I could still be useful to my country. But love counseled me, with no less force, to stay near

Marie, to be her protector and champion. Although I foresaw a near and inevitable change in the march of events, still I could not, without trembling, contemplate the danger of her position.

My reflections were interrupted by the entrance of a Cossack, who came to announce that the "great Czar" called me to his presence. "Where is he?" I asked, preparing to obey. "In the commandant's house," replied the Cossack. "After dinner the Czar went to the vapor baths. It must be confessed that all his ways are imperial! He can do more than others; at dinner he deigned to eat two roast milk-pigs; afterward at the bath he endured the highest degree of heat; even the attendant could not stand it; he handed the brush to another and was restored to consciousness only by the application of cold water. It is said that in the bath, the marks of the true Czar were plainly seen on his breast—a picture of his own face and a double-headed eagle."

I did not think it necessary to contradict the Cossack, and I followed him to the Commandant's, trying to fancy in advance my interview with Pougatcheff, and its result. The reader may imagine that I was not quite at ease. Night was falling as I reached the house. The gibbet with its victims still stood, black and terrible. The poor body of our good Basilia was lying under the steps, near which two Cossacks mounted guard. He who had brought me, entered to announce my arrival; he returned at once, and led me to the room where the evening before I had taken leave of Marie. At a table covered with a cloth, and laden with bottles and glasses, sat Pougatcheff, surrounded by some ten Cossack chiefs in colored caps and shirts, with flushed faces and sparkling eyes, the effect, no doubt, of the wine-cup.

I saw neither of our traitors, Alexis or the Corporal, amongst them.

"Ah! your lordship, it is you?" said their chief, on seeing me. "Be welcome! Honor and place at the table!"

The guests drew closer together. I took a place at the end of the table. My neighbor, a young Cossack of slender form and handsome face, poured out a bumper of brandy for me. I did not taste it. I was busy considering the assembly. Pougatcheff was seated in the place of honor, elbow on table, his heavy, black beard resting upon his muscular hand. His features, regular and handsome, had no ferocious expression. He often spoke to a man of some fifty years, calling him now Count, again Uncle. All treated each other as comrades, showing no very marked deference for their chief. They talked of the assault that morning; of the revolt, its success, and of their next operations. Each one boasted of his prowess, gave his opinions, and freely contradicted Pougatcheff. In this strange council of war, they resolved to march upon Orenbourg, a bold move, but justified by previous successes. The departure was fixed for the next day. Each one drank another bumper, and rising, took leave of Pougatcheff. I wished to follow them, but the brigand said: "Wait, I want to speak to you."

Pougatcheff looked at me fixedly in silence for a few seconds, winking his left eye with the most cunning, mocking expression. At last he burst into a long peal of laughter, so hearty, that I, just from seeing him, began to laugh, without knowing why.

"Well, my lord," said he, "confess that you were frightened, when my boys put the rope around your neck? The sky must have seemed to you then as big as a sheep-skin. And if not for your servant, you would have been swinging up there from the cross-beam; but at that very instant I recognized the old owl. Would you have thought that the man who led you to a shelter on the steppe was the great Czar himself?" Saying these words, he assumed a grave and mysterious air. "You have been very guilty," continued he, "but I have pardoned you, for having done me a kindness, when I was obliged to hide from my enemies. I shall load you with favors, when I shall have regained my empire. Do you promise to serve me with zeal?"

The bandit's question and impudence made me smile.

"Why do you laugh?" said he, frowning, "do you not believe that I am the great Czar? Answer frankly."

I was troubled. I could not recognize a vagabond as the emperor; to call him an impostor to his face was to doom myself to death; and the sacrifice which I was ready to make under the gibbet that morning, before all the people, in the first flush of indignation, seemed now a useless bravado. Pougatcheff awaited my answer in fierce silence. At last (I still remember with satisfaction that duty triumphed over human weakness) I replied to Pougatcheff.

"I will tell you the truth and let you decide. Should I reco-gnize you as the Czar, as you are a man of intelligence, you would see that I am lying."

"Then who am I? in your opinion."

"God knows, but whoever you are, you are playing a dangerous game."

Pougatcheff gave me a sharp, quick glance. "You do not believe that I am the emperor, Peter III? Be it so. Have not bold men succeeded before me and obtained the crown? Think what you please about me, but stay with me. What matters it whom you serve? Success is right. Serve under me, and I will make you a field-marshal, a prince. What say you?"

"No," said I. "I am a nobleman. I have taken an oath to her majesty, the Empress; I can not serve with you. If truly you wish me well, send me to Orenbourg."

Pougatcheff reflected. "If I send you there, you will, at least, promise not to bear arms against me?"

"How can I promise that? If I am ordered to march against you, I must go. You are now a chief; you desire your subordinates to obey you. No, my life is in your hand; if you give me liberty, thanks; if you put me to death, may God judge you."

My frankness pleased him. "Be it so," said he, slapping me on the shoulders, "pardon or punish to the end. You can go the four quarters of the world, and do as you like. Come tomorrow, and bid me good-bye. Now go to bed—I require rest myself."

I went out into the street. The night was clear and cold; the moon and stars shone out in all their brightness, lighting up the square and the gibbet. All was quiet and dark in the rest of the fortress. At the inn some lights were visible, and belated drinkers broke the stillness by their shouts. I glanced at Accoulina's house; the doors and windows were closed, and all seemed perfectly quiet there. I went to my room, and found Saveliitch deploring my absence. I told him of my freedom. "Thanks to thee, O

God!" said he, making the sign of the cross; "tomorrow we shall set out at daybreak. I have prepared something for you; eat and then sleep till morning, tranquil as if in the bosom of the Good Shepherd."

I followed his advice, and after having supped, fell asleep on the bare floor, as fatigued in mind as in body.

IX

THE SEPARATION

The drum awoke me early the next morning. I went out on the square. Pougatcheff's troops were there, falling into rank, around the gibbet, to which still hung the victims of yesterday. The Cossacks were mounted; the infantry and artillery, with our single gun, were accoutred ready for the march. The inhabitants were also assembled there awaiting the usurper. Before the steps of the Commandant's house a Cossack held by the bridle a magnificent white horse. My eyes sought the body of our good Basilia. It had been dragged aside and covered with an old bark mat. At last Pougatcheff came out on the steps, and saluted the crowd. All heads were bared. One of the chiefs handed him a bag of copper coin, which he threw by the handful among the people. Perceiving me in the crowd, he signed to me to approach.

"Listen," said he, "go at once to Orenbourg, and say from me, to the Governor and all the Generals, that I shall be there in a week. Counsel them to receive me with submission and filial love, otherwise they shall not escape the direst torture. A pleasant journey to you." The principal followers of Pougatcheff surrounded him, Alexis amongst others. The usurper turned to the people, and

Alexander Pushkin

pointing to Alexis, said: "Behold your new Commandant; obey him in every thing; he is responsible for you and for the fortress."

The words made me shudder. What would become of Marie? Pougatcheff descended the steps and vaulted quickly into his saddle without the aid of his attendant Cossacks. At that moment Saveliitch came out of the crowd, approached the usurper, and presented him a sheet of paper.

"What is this?" asked Pougatcheff, with dignity.

"Read, you will deign to see," replied the serf.

Pougatcheff examined the paper. "You write very illegibly; where is my Secretary?"

A boy in corporal's uniform came running to the brigand. "Read aloud," said he. I was curious to know for what purpose the old man had written to Pougatcheff. The Secretary began to spell out in a loud voice what follows:

"Two dressing-gowns, one in percale, the other in striped silk, six roubles."

"What does this mean?" said Pougatcheff, frowning.

"Command him to read on," replied Saveliitch, with perfect calmness.

The Secretary continued: "One uniform in fine green cloth, seven roubles; one pair of white cloth pantaloons, five roubles; twelve shirts of Holland linen, with cuffs, ten roubles; one case containing a tea-service, two roubles."

"What nonsense is this?" said Pougatcheff.

"What have I to do with tea-sets and Holland cuffs?"

Saveliitch coughed to clear his voice, and began to explain: "That, my lord, deign to understand, is the bill of my master's goods carried off by the thieves."

"What thieves?" asked Pougatcheff, with a terrible air.

"Pardon me," said Saveliitch. "Thieves? No, they were not thieves; my tongue slipped; yet your boys went through everything and carried off plenty. That can not be denied. Do not be angry. The horse has four legs and yet he stumbles. Command that he read to the end."

"Well, read," said Pougatcheff.

"One Persian blanket, one quilt of wadded silk, four roubles; one pelisse of fox-skin, covered with red ratine, forty roubles; one small touloup of hare-skin left with your grace, on the steppe, fifteen roubles."

"What?" cried Pougatcheff, with flashing eyes.

I must say I feared for the old man, who was beginning new explanations, when the brigand interrupted him:

"How dare you annoy me with these trifles?" said he, snatching the paper from the Secretary and throwing it in the old man's face. "You have been despoiled! old fool! great harm! You ought to thank God that you are not hanging up there, with the other rebels, both you and your master. I'll give you a hare-skin touloup! Do you know that I will have you flayed alive, that touloups may be made of you?"

Alexander Pushkin

"As you please," replied Saveliitch; "but I am not a free man, and I am responsible for my master's goods."

Pougatcheff, who was evidently playing the magnanimous, turned his head and set off without a word. Alexis and the other chiefs followed him. The whole army left the fortress in good order, the people forming an escort. I stayed alone on the square with Saveliitch, who held in his hand the bill and considered it with deep regret. I could not help laughing.

"Laugh, my lord, laugh, but when the household is to be furnished again, we shall see if it be a laughing matter."

I went to learn of Marie Mironoff. Accoulina met me and told me a sad piece of news. During the night a burning fever had seized the poor girl. Accoulina took me into her chamber. The invalid was delirious and did not recognize me. I was shocked by the change in her countenance. The position of this sorrowing orphan, without defenders, alarmed me as much as my inability to protect grieved me. Alexis, above all, was to be feared. Chief, invested with the usurper's authority, in the fortress with this unhappy girl, he was capable of any crime. What ought I to do to deliver her? To set out at once for Orenbourg, to hasten the deliverance of Belogorsk, and to co-operate in it, if possible. I took leave of Father Garasim and Accoulina, recommending to them Marie, who I already looked upon as my wife. I kissed the young girl's hand, and left the room.

"Adieu, Peter Grineff," said Accoulina. "Do not forget us. Except you, Marie has no support or consolation." Choked by emotion, I did not reply. Out on the square, I stopped an instant before the gibbet. With bare head I reverently saluted the loyal dead, and took the road to

Orenbourg, accompanied by Saveliitch, who would not abandon me. Thus plunged in thought, I walked on. Hearing horses galloping behind me, I turned my head and saw a Cossack from the fortress leading a horse, and making signs to me that I should wait. I recognized our Corporal. Having caught up with us, he dismounted from his own horse, and giving me the bridle of the other, said: "Our Czar makes you a gift of a horse, and a pelisse from his own shoulder." To the saddle was tied a sheep-skin touloup. I put it on, mounted the horse, taking Saveliitch up behind me. "You see, my lord," said my serf, "that my petition to the bandit was not useless! And although this old hack and this peasant's touloup are not worth half what the rascals stole, yet they are better than nothing. 'A worthless dog yields even a handful of hair.'"

X

THE SIEGE

Approaching Orenbourg, we saw a crowd of convicts, with shaved heads and faces disfigured by the pincers of the public executioner. At that time red-hot irons were applied to tear out the nostrils of the condemned. They were working at the fortifications of the place under the supervision of the garrison pensioners. Some carried away in wheel-barrows the rubbish that filled the ditch, others threw up the earth, while masons were examining and repairing the walls. The sentry stopped us at the gate and asked for our passports. When the sergeant heard that we were from Belogorsk he took me at once to the General, who was in his garden. I found him examining the apple trees, which autumnal winds had already despoiled of their leaves; assisted by an old gardener, he covered them carefully with straw. His face expressed calmness, good humor and health. He seemed very glad to see me, and questioned me about the terrible events I had witnessed. The old man heard me attentively, and whilst listening, cut off the dead branches.

"Poor Mironoff!" said he, when I had finished my story; "it is a pity; he was a brave officer; and Madame Mironoff a kind lady, an expert in pickling mushrooms. What has become of Marie, the Captain's daughter?"

"She is in the fortress, at the house of the Greek priest."

"Aye! aye! aye!" exclaimed the General. "That's bad, very bad; for it is impossible to depend upon the discipline of brigands."

I observed that the fortress of Belogorsk was not far off, and that probably his Excellency would send a detachment of troops to deliver the poor inhabitants.

The General shook his head, doubtfully. "We shall see! we shall see! there is plenty of time to talk about it; come, I beg you, to take tea with me. Tonight there will be a council of war; you can give us some precise information regarding this Pougatcheff and his army. Meantime, go and rest."

I went to my allotted quarters, where I found Saveliitch already installed. I awaited impatiently the hour indicated, and the reader may believe that I did not fail to be present at this council, which was to influence my whole life. I found at the General's a custom- house officer, the Director, as well as I can remember a little old man, red-faced and fat, wearing a robe of black watered silk. He questioned me about the fate of the Captain Mironoff, whom he called his chum, and often interrupted me by sententious remarks, which, if they did not prove him to be a man well versed in war, showed his natural intelligence and shrewdness. During this time other guests arrived. When all had taken their places, and to each had been offered a cup of tea, the General carefully stated the questions to be considered.

"Now, gentlemen," said he, "we must decide what action

is to be taken against the rebels. Shall we act offensively, or defensively? Each of these ways has its advantages and disadvantages. Offensive war presents more hope of a rapid extermination of the enemy, but defensive war is safer and offers fewer dangers. Let us then take the vote in legal order; that is, consult first the youngest in rank. Ensign," continued he, addressing me, "deign to give your opinion."

I rose, and in a few words depicted Pougatcheff and his army. I affirmed that the usurper was not in a condition to resist disciplined forces. My opinion was received by the civil service employes with visible discontent. They saw nothing in it but the levity of a young man. A murmur arose, and I heard distinctly the word "hare-brained" murmured in a low voice. The General turned to me smiling, and said:

"Ensign, the first votes (the youngest) in war councils, are for offensive measures. Now let us continue to collect the votes. The College Director will give us his opinion."

The little old man in black silk, a College Director, as well as a customs officer, swallowed his third cup of tea, well dashed with a strong dose of rum, and hastened to speak:

"Your Excellency," said he, "I think that we ought to act neither offensively nor defensively."

"What's that, sir?" said the General, stupefied; "military tactics present no other means; we must act either offensively or defensively."

"Your Excellency, act *subornatively.*"

"Eh! eh! Your opinion is judicious," said the General; "subornative acts—that is to say, indirect acts—are also admitted by the science of tactics, and we will profit by your counsel. We might offer for the rascal's head seventy or even a hundred roubles, to be taken out of the secret funds."

"And then," interrupted the man in silk, "may I be a Kirghis ram, instead of a College Director, if the thieves do not bring their chief to you, chained hand and foot."

"We can think about it," said the General. "But let us, in any case, take some military measures. Gentlemen, give your votes in legal order."

All the opinions were contrary to mine. All agreed, that it was better to stay behind a strong stone wall, protected by cannon, than to tempt fortune in the open field. Finally, when all the opinions were known, the General shook the ashes from his pipe and pronounced the following discourse:

"Gentlemen, I am of the Ensign's opinion, for it is according to the science of military tactics, which always prefers offensive movements to defensive." He stopped and stuffed the tobacco into his pipe. I glanced exultingly at the civil service employes, who, with discontented looks, were whispering to each other.

"But, gentlemen," continued he, giving out with a sigh a long puff of smoke, "I dare not assume the responsibility. I go with the majority, which has decided that we await in this city the threatened siege, and repulse the enemy by the power of artillery, and if possible, by well-directed sorties."

Alexander Pushkin

The council broke up. I could not but deplore the weakness of the worthy soldier, who, contrary to his own convictions, decided to follow the opinion of ignorant inexperience.

Some days after this famous council of war, Pougatcheff, true to his word, approached Orenbourg. From the top of the city walls I made a reconnaissance of the rebel army. It seemed to me that their number had increased ten-fold. They had more artillery, taken from the small forts captured by Pougatcheff. Remembering our council, I foresaw a long captivity behind the walls of Orenbourg, and I was ready to cry with chagrin. Far from me the intention of describing the siege of Orenbourg, which belongs to history and not to family memoirs. Suffice it to say, that this siege was disastrous to the inhabitants, who had to suffer hunger and privations of every kind. Life at Orenbourg became insupportable. The decision of fate was awaited with anguish. Food was scarce; bombshells fell upon the defenseless houses of citizens. The attacks of Pougatcheff made very little excitement. I was dying of *ennui*. I had promised Accoulina that I would correspond with her, but communication was cut off, and I could not send or receive a letter from Belogorsk. My only pastime consisted in military sorties. Thanks to Pougatcheff I had an excellent horse, and I shared my meager pittance with it. I went out every day beyond the ramparts to skirmish with Pougatcheff's advance guards. The rebels had the best of it; they had plenty of food and were well mounted. Our poor cavalry were in no condition to oppose them. Sometimes our half-starved infantry went into the field; but the depth of the snow hindered them from acting successfully against the flying cavalry of the enemy. The artillery vainly thundered from the ramparts, and in the field it could not advance, because of the weakness of our attenuated horses. This was our way of making war; this is what the civil service employes of Orenbourg called prudence and foresight.

One day when we had routed and driven before us quite a large troop, I overtook a straggling Cossack; my Turkish sabre was uplifted to strike him when he doffed his cap and cried out: "Good day, Peter, how fares your health?"

I recognized our Corporal. I was delighted to see him.

"Good day, Maxim. How long since you left Belogorsk?"

"Not long, Peter. I came yesterday. I have a letter for you."

"Where is it?" I cried, delighted.

"Here," replied Maxim, putting his hand in his bosom. "I promised Polacca to try and give it to you." He gave me a folded paper, and set off on a gallop. I read with agitation the following lines:

"By the will of God I am deprived of my parents, and except you, Peter, I know of no one who can protect me; Alexis commands in place of my late father. He so terrified Father Garasim that I was obliged to go and live at our house, where I am cruelly treated by Alexis. He will force me to become his wife. He says he saved my life by not betraying the trick of passing for the niece of Accoulina. I could rather die than be his wife. I have three days to accept his offer; after that I need expect no mercy from him. O, Peter! entreat your General to send us help, and if possible, come yourself.

MARIE MIRONOFF."

This letter nearly crazed me. I rushed back to the city, not sparing the spur to my poor horse. A thousand projects flashed through my mind to rescue her. Arrived in the city, I hurried to the General's and ran into his room. He was walking up and down smoking his meerschaum. Seeing me he stopped, alarmed at my abrupt entrance.

"Your Excellency, I come to you, as to my own father; do not refuse me; the happiness of my life depends upon it."

"But what is it?" said the General; "what can I do for you?"

"Your Excellency, permit me to take a battalion of soldiers and half a hundred Cossacks, to go and storm the fortress of Belogorsk."

"Storm the fortress?" said the General.

"I answer for the success of the attack, only let me go."

"No, young man," said he; "at so great a distance the enemy would easily cut off all communication with the principal strategic point."

I was frightened by his military wisdom, and hastened to interrupt him: "Captain Mironoff's daughter has written me, begging for relief. Alexis threatens to compel her to be his wife!"

"Ah! Alexis, traitor! If he fall into my hands I shall try him in twenty-four hours, and he shall be shot on the glacis of the fortress! meantime patience."

"Patience!" I cried; "in the interval Marie will be compelled to obey him."

"Oh," said the General, "that would not be a misfortune—it is better that she should become the wife of Alexis, who can protect her. When we shall have shot the traitor, then she will find a better husband."

"I would rather die," I said with fury, "than yield her to Alexis."

"I understand it all now," said the old man. "You are, no doubt, in love yourself with Marie Mironoff. That's another thing. Poor boy! Still, I can not give you a battalion and fifty Cossacks. The thing is unreasonable." I hung my head in despair. But I had a plan of my own.

Alexander Pushkin

XI

THE REBEL CAMP

I left the General and hastened to my quarters. Saveliitch received me with his usual remonstrance: "What pleasure, my lord, is there in fighting these drunken brigands? If they were Turks or Swedes, all right; but these sons of dogs—"

I interrupted him: "How much money have I in all?"

"You have plenty," said he with a satisfied air. "I knew how to whisk it out of sight of the rogues." He drew from his pocket a long knitted purse full of silver coin.

"Saveliitch, give me half of what you have there, and keep the rest for yourself. I am off for the fortress of Belogorsk."

"Oh, Peter!" said the old serf, "do you not fear God? The roads are cut off. Have pity on your parents; wait a little; our troops will come and disperse the brigands, and then you can go to the four quarters of the world."

"It is too late to reflect. I must go. Do not grieve, Saveliitch; I make you a present of that money. Buy what you need. If I do not return in three days—"

"My dear," said the old man, "I will go with you, were it on foot. If you go, I must first lose my senses before I will stay crouching behind stone walls."

There was never any use disputing with the old man. In half an hour I was in the saddle, Saveliitch on an old, half-starved, limping rosinante, which a citizen, not having fodder, had given for nothing to the serf. We reached the city gates; the sentinels let us pass, and we were finally out of Orenbourg. Night was falling. My road lay before the town of Berd, the headquarters of Pougatcheff. This road was blocked up and hidden by snow; but across the steppe were traces of horses, renewed from day to day, apparently, and clearly visible. I was going at a gallop, Saveliitch could scarcely keep up and shouted, "Not so fast! My nag can not follow yours." Very soon we saw the lights of Berd. We were approaching deep ravines, which served as natural fortifications to the town. Saveliitch, without however being left behind, never ceased his lamentations. I was in hopes of passing safely the enemy's place, when I saw through the darkness five peasants armed with big sticks—Pougatcheff's extreme outpost.

"*Qui vive*! Who goes there?"

Not knowing the watchword, I was for going on without answering. But one of them seized my horse's bridle. I drew my sabre and struck the peasant of the head. His cap saved his life; he staggered and fell; the others, frightened, let me pass. The darkness, which was deepening, might have saved me from further hindrance; when, looking back, I saw that Saveliitch was not with me. What was I to do? The poor old man, with his lame horse, could not escape from the rascals. I waited a minute; then, sure

Alexander Pushkin

that they must have seized him, I turned my horse's head to go and aid him. Approaching the ravine I heard voices, and recognized that of Saveliitch. Hastening my steps, was soon within sight of the peasants. They had dismounted the old man, and were about to garrote him. They rushed upon me; in an instant I was on foot. Their chief said I should be conducted to the Czar. I made no resistance. We crossed the ravine to enter the town, which was illuminated. The streets were crowded and noisy. We were taken to a hut on the corner of two streets. There were some barrels of wine and a cannon near the door. One of the peasants said: "Here is the palace; we will announce you." I glanced at Saveliitch; he was making signs of the cross, and praying. We waited a long time. At last the peasant re-appeared and said: "The Czar orders the officers to his presence."

The palace, as the peasant called it, was lighted by two tallow candles. The walls were hung with gold paper. But every thing else, the benches, the table, the basin hung up by a cord, the towel on a nail in the wall, the shelf laden with earthen vessels, were exactly the same as in any other cabin. Pougatcheff, wearing his scarlet cafetan and high Cossack cap, with his hand on his hip, sat beneath the sacred pictures common to every Russian abode. Around him stood several of his chiefs. I could see that the arrival of an officer from Orenbourg had awakened some curiosity, and that they had prepared to receive me with pomp. Pougatcheff recognized me at once, and his assumed gravity disappeared.

"Ah! it is your lordship! how are you? What brings you here?"

I replied that I was traveling about my private business, when his people arrested me.

"What business?" asked he. I did not know what to answer. Pougatcheff thinking that I would not speak before witnesses gave a sign to his comrades to leave. All obeyed except two. "Speak before these," said he; "conceal nothing from them."

I glanced at these intimates of the usurper. One was an old man frail and bent, remarkable for nothing but a blue riband crossed over his coarse gray cloth cafetan; but I shall never forget his companion. He was tall, of powerful build, and seemed about forty-five. A thick red beard, piercing gray eyes, a nose without nostrils, marks of the searing irons on his forehead and cheeks, gave to his broad face, pitted by small-pox a most fierce expression. He wore a red shirt, a Kirghis robe, and wide Cossack pantaloons. Although wholly pre- occupied by my own feelings, yet this company deeply impressed me. Pougatcheff recalled me to myself quickly.

"What business brought you from Orenbourg?"

A bold idea suggested itself to my mind. It seemed to me that Providence, leading me a second time before this robber, gave me the means of accomplishing my work. I decided to seize the chance, and without reflecting on the step, I replied:

"I am on the way to the fortress of Belogorsk to liberate an oppressed orphan there."

Pougatcheff's eyes flashed. "Who dares to oppress an orphan? Were he seven feet high, he shall not escape my vengeance. Speak, who is the guilty one?"

"Alexis; he holds in slavery that same young girl whom you saw at Father Garasim's, and wants to force her to marry him."

"I shall give Alexis a lesson! I'll teach him to oppress my subjects. I shall hang him."

"Permit me a word," said the man without nostrils. "You were too hasty giving the command to Alexis. You offended the Cossacks by giving them a noble as chief; do not offend the gentlemen by hanging one of them on the first accusation."

"There is no need to pardon nor pity," said the man with the blue riband. "It would be no harm to hang Alexis, nor to question this gentleman. Why does he visit us? If he does not acknowledge you as Czar he has no justice to get at your hands; if he acknowledge you, why did he stay at Orenbourg with your enemies? Will you not order him to prison, and have a fire lighted there?"

The old rascal's logic seemed plausible even to myself. I shuddered when I remembered into whose hands I had fallen. Pougatcheff saw my trouble.

"Eh! eh! your lordship," said he, winking, "it seems my field-marshal is right. What do you think?"

The jesting tone of the chief restored my courage. I replied calmly that I was in his power.

"Well," said Pougatcheff, "tell me now the condition of your city?"

"It is, thank God, in a good state."

"A good condition," repeated the brigand, "when the people are dying of hunger."

The usurper was right, but according to the duty imposed by my oath, I affirmed that it was a false report, and that the fort was sufficiently provisioned.

"You see he deceives you," interrupted the man with the riband. "All the deserters are unanimous in saying that famine and pestilence are at Orenbourg; that thistles are eaten as dainties there. If you wish to hang Alexis, hang on the same gibbet this young fellow, that they may be equal."

These words seemed to shake the chief. Happily the other wretch opposed this view.

"Silence," said this powerful fellow. "You think of nothing but hanging and strangling. It becomes *you* to play the hero. To look at you, no one knows where your soul is."

"And which of the saints are you?" replied the old man.

"Generals," said Pougatcheff, with dignity, "an end to your quarrels. It would be no great loss if all the mangy dogs from Orenbourg were dangling their legs under the same cross-beam; but it would be a misfortune if our own good dogs should bite each other."

Feeling the necessity of changing the conversation, I turned to Pougatcheff with a smile, and said:

"Ah! I forgot to thank you for the horse and touloup. Without your aid I should not have reached the city. I would have died from cold on the journey." My trick succeeded. Pougatcheff regained his good humor.

"The beauty of debt is the payment thereof," said he,

winking. "Tell me your story. What have you to do with the young girl that Alexis persecutes? Has she caught your heart, too?"

"She is my promised bride" said I, seeing no risk in speaking the truth.

"Your promised bride! Why did you not tell me sooner? We'll marry you, and be at your wedding. Listen, Field-marshal," said he. "We are old friends, his lordship and I. Lets us go to supper. Tomorrow we shall see what is to be done with him. Night brings wisdom, and the morning is better than the evening."

I would gladly have excused myself from proposed honor, but it was impossible. Two Cossacks girls covered the table with a white cloth, and brought bread, soup made of fish, and pitchers of wine and beer. Thus, for the second time, I was at table with Pougatcheff and his terrible companions. The orgie lasted far into the night. Drunkenness at last triumphed. Pougatcheff fell asleep in his place, and his companions signed to me to leave him. I went out with them. The sentry locked me up in a dark hole, where I found Saveliitch. He was so surprised by all that he saw and heard, that he asked no questions. Lying in darkness, he soon fell asleep.

The next morning Pougatcheff sent for me. Before his door stood a kibitka, with three horses abreast. The street was crowded. Pougatcheff, whom I met in the entry of his hut, was dressed for a journey, in a pelisse and Kirghis cap. His guests of the previous night surrounded him, and wore a look of submission which contrasted strongly with what I had seen on the preceding evening. Pougatcheff bade me good-morning gaily, and ordered me to sit beside him in the kibitka. We took our places.

"To the fortress of Belogorsk," said Pougatcheff to the robust Tartar, who, standing, drove his horses. My heart beat violently. The Tartar horses shot off, the bells tinkled, the kibitka flew over the snow.

"Stop! stop!" cried a voice I knew too well. "O Peter! do not abandon me in my old age, in the midst of the rob—"

"Ah, you old owl!" said Pougatcheff, "sit up there in front."

"Thanks, Czar, may God give you a long life."

The horses set off again. The people in the streets stopped and bowed low, as the usurper passed. Pougatcheff saluted right and left. In an instant we were out of the town, taking our way over a well-defined road. I was silent. Pougatcheff broke in upon my reverie. "Why so silent, my lord?" said he.

"I can not help thinking," said I, "of the chain of events. I am an officer, noble, yesterday at war with you; today I ride in the same carriage with you, and all the happiness of my life depends on you."

"Are you afraid?"

"You have already given me my life!"

"You say truly. You know how my fellows looked upon you; only today they wanted to try you as a spy. The old one wanted to torture and then hang you; but I would not, because I remembered your glass of wine and your touloup. I am not bloodthirsty, as your friends say." I remembered the taking of our fortress, but I did not contradict him.

"What do they say of me at Orenbourg?"

"It is said there, that you will not be easily vanquished. It must be confessed that you have given us some work."

"Yes; I am a great warrior. Do you think the King Prussia is as strong as I?"

"What do you think yourself? Can you beat Frederick?"

"Frederick the Great? Why not? Wait till I march to Moscow!"

"You really intend to march on Moscow?"

"God knows," said he, reflecting; "my road is narrow— my boys do not obey—they are thieves—I must listen— keep my ears open; at the first reverse they would save their own necks by my head."

"Would it not be better," I said, "to abandon them now, before it is too late, and have recourse to the clemency of the Empress?"

He smiled bitterly. "No; the time is passed. I shall end as I began. Who knows?"

Our Tartar was humming a plaintive air; Saveliitch, sound asleep, swayed from side to side; our kibitka was gliding rapidly over the winter road. I saw in the distance a village well known to my eyes, with its palisade and church spire on the steep bank of the river Iaik. A quarter of an hour after we entered the fortress of Belogorsk.

XII

MARIE

The kibitka stopped before the Commandant's house. The inhabitants had recognized the usurper's bells and equipage, and had come out in crowds to meet him. Alexis, dressed like a Cossack, and bearded like one, helped the brigand to descend from his kibitka. The sight of me troubled him, but soon recovering himself, he said: "You are one of us?" I turned my head away without replying. My heart was wrung when we entered the room that I know so well, where still upon the wall hung, like an epitaph, the diploma of the deceased Commandant. Pougatcheff seated himself upon the same sofa where many a time Ivan Mironoff had dozed to the hum of his wife's voice. Alexis' own hand presented the brandy to his chief. Pougatcheff drank a glass and said, pointing to me: "Offer a glass to his lordship." Alexis approached me, and again I turned my back upon him. Pougatcheff asked him a few questions about the condition of the fortress, and then, in an unpremeditated manner, said: "Tell me, who is this young girl that you have under guard?"

Alexis became pale as death. "Czar," said he, a tremor in his voice, "she is in her own room; she is not locked up."

Alexander Pushkin

"Take me to her room," said the usurper, rising.

Hesitation was impossible. Alexis led the way to Marie's room. I followed. On the stairs Alexis stopped: "Czar, demand of me what you will, but do not permit a stranger to enter my wife's room."

"You are married?" I shouted, ready to tear him to pieces.

"Silence!" interrupted the brigand, "this is my business. And you," said he, turning to Alexis, "do not be too officious. Whether she be your wife or not, I shall take whom I please into her room. Your lordship, follow me."

At the door of the room Alexis stopped again: "Czar, she has had a fever these three days; she is delirious."

"Open," said Pougatcheff.

Alexis fumbled in his pockets, and at last said that he had forgotten the key. Pougatcheff kicked the door; the lock yielded, the door opened and we entered.

I glanced into the room, and nearly fainted. On the floor, in the coarse dress of a peasant, Marie was seated, pale, thin, her hair in disorder; before her on the floor stood a pitcher of water covered by a piece of bread. Upon seeing me, she started, and uttered a piercing shriek. Pougatcheff glanced at Alexis, smiled bitterly, and said: "Your hospital is in nice order?"

"Tell me, my little dove, why does your husband punish you in this way?"

"My husband! he is not my husband. I am resolved to die rather than marry him; and I shall die, if not soon released."

Pougatcheff gave a furious look at Alexis, and said: "Do you dare to deceive me, knave?"

Alexis fell on his knees. Contempt stifled all my feelings of hatred and vengeance. I saw with disgust, a gentleman kneeling at the feet of a Cossack deserter.

"I pardon you, this time," said the brigand, "but remember, your next fault will recall this one." He turned to Marie, and said, gently: "Come out, my pretty girl, you are free. I am the Czar!"

Marie looked at him, hid her face in her hands and fell on the floor unconscious. She had no doubt divined that he had caused her parents' death. I rushed to aid her, when my old acquaintance, Polacca, boldly entered, and hastened to revive her mistress. Pougatcheff, Alexis and I went down to the reception room.

"Now, your lordship, we have released the pretty girl, what say you? Shall we not send for Father Garasim, and have him perform the marriage ceremony for his niece? If you like, I will be your father by proxy, Alexis your groomsman; then we'll shut the gates and make merry!"

As I anticipated, Alexis, hearing this speech, lost his self-control.

"Czar," said he, in a fury, "I am guilty; I have lied to you, but Grineff also deceives you. This young girl is not Father Garasim's niece. She is Ivan Mironoff's daughter."

Pougatcheff glared at me. "What does that mean?" said he to me.

"Alexis says truly," I replied, firmly.

"You did not tell me that," said the usurper, whose face darkened.

"Judge of it yourself. Could I declare before your people that Marie was Captain Mironoff's daughter? They would have torn her to pieces. No one could have saved her."

"You are right," said Pougatcheff, "my drunkards would not have spared the child. Accoulina did well to deceive them."

"Listen," I said, seeing his good humor, "I do not know your real name, and I do not want to know it. But before God, I am ready to pay you with my life, for what you have done for me. Only, ask me nothing contrary to honor, and my conscience as a Christian. You are my benefactor. Let me go with this orphan, and we, whatever happens to you, wherever you may be, we shall pray God to save your soul."

"Be it as you desire," said he, "punish to the end, or pardon completely, that's my way. Take your promised bride wherever you choose, and may God give you love and happiness." He turned to Alexis, and ordered him to write me a passport for all the forts subject to his power. Alexis was petrified with astonishment. Pougatcheff went off to inspect the fortress; Alexis followed him; I remained.

I ran up to Marie's room. The door was closed. I knocked.

"Who is there?" asked Polacca.

I gave my name. I heard Marie say: "In an instant, Peter, I shall join you at Accoulina's."

Father Garasim and Accoulina came out to welcome me. I was honored with everything at the command of the hostess, whose voluble tongue never ceased. It was not long before Marie entered, quite pale; she had laid aside the peasant's dress, and was, as usual, clad in simplicity, but with neatness and taste. I seized her hand, unable to utter a word. We were both silent from full hearts. Our hosts left us, and I could now speak of plans for her safety. It was impossible that she should stay in a fortress subject to Pougatcheff, and commanded by the infamous Alexis. Neither could she find refuge at Orenbourg, suffering all the horrors of siege. I proposed that she should go to my father's country-seat. This surprised her. But I assured her that my father would hold it a duty and an honor to receive the daughter of a veteran who had died for his country. In conclusion, I said: "My dear Marie; I consider thee as my wife; these strange events have bound us for ever to each other."

Marie listened with dignity; she felt as I did, but repeated that without my parents' consent she would never be my wife. I could not reply to this objection. I folded her to my heart, and my project became our mutual resolve.

An hour after, the Corporal brought me my passport, having the scratch which served as Pougatcheff's sign-manual, and told me that the Czar awaited me. I found him ready for his journey. To this man—why not tell the truth?—cruel and terrible to all but me, I was drawn by strong sympathy. I wanted to snatch him from the horde of robbers, whose chief he was; but the presence of Alexis and the crowd around him prevented any expression of these feelings. Our parting was that of friends. As the horses were moving, he leaned out of the kibitka and said to me: "Adieu, again, your lordship; perhaps we may meet once more."

Alexander Pushkin

We did meet again, but under what circumstances!

I returned to Father Garasim's, where our preparations were soon completed. Our baggage was put into the Commandant's old equipage. The horses were harnessed. Marie went, before setting off, to visit once more the tomb in the church-yard, and soon returned, having wept in silence over all that remained to her of her parents. Father Garasim and Accoulina stood on the steps. Marie, Polacca, and I sat in the interior of the kibitka. Saveliitch perched himself up in front.

"Adieu, Marie, sweet little dove! Adieu, Peter, our handsome falcon!" exclaimed the kind Accoulina.

Passing the Commandant's house, I saw Alexis, whose face expressed determined hate.

XIII

THE ARREST

In two hours we reached the neighboring fortress, which also belonged to Pougatcheff. We there changed horses. By the celerity with which they served us, and the eager zeal of the bearded Cossack, whom Pougatcheff had made Commandant, I perceived that, thanks to the talk of our postilion, I was supposed to be a favorite with their master. When we started off again, it was dusk; we were drawing near a town where, according to the bearded Commandant, there ought to be a very strong detachment of Pougatcheff's forces. The sentinels stopped us and to the demand: "Who goes there?" our postilion answered in a loud voice: "A friend of the Czar, traveling with his wife."

We were at once surrounded by a detachment of Russian hussars, who swore frightfully.

"Come out," said a Russian officer, heavily mustached; "We'll give you a bath!"

I requested to be taken before the authorities. Perceiving that I was an officer, the soldiers ceased swearing, and the officer took me to the Major's. Saveliitch followed,

Alexander Pushkin

growling out: "We fall from the fire into the flame!"

The kibitka came slowly after us. In five minutes we reached a small house, all lighted up. The officer left me under a strong guard, and entered to announce my capture. He returned almost instantly, saying that I was ordered to prison, and her ladyship to the presence of the Major.

"Is he mad?" I cried.

"I can not tell, your lordship."

I jumped up the steps—the sentinels had not time to stop me—and burst into the room where six hussar officers were playing faro. The Major kept the bank. I instantly recognized the Major as Ivan Zourine, who had so thoroughly emptied my purse at Simbirsk. "Is it possible? is this you Ivan Zourine?"

"Halloo! Peter; what luck? where are you from? will you take a chance?"

"Thanks; I would rather have some apartments assigned me."

"No need of apartments, stay with me."

"I can not; I am not alone."

"Bring your comrade with you."

"I am not with a comrade; I am with—a lady."

"A lady! where did you fish her out?" and he whistled in so rollicking a manner, that the rest burst out laughing.

"Well," said Zourine, "then you must have a house in the town. Here, boy! why do you not bring in Pougatcheff's friend?"

"What are you about," said I. "It is Captain Mironoff's daughter. I have just obtained her liberty, and I am taking her to my father's, where I shall leave her."

"In the name of Heaven, what are *you* talking about? Are *you* Pougatcheff's chum?"

"I will tell you everything later; first go and see this poor girl, whom your soldiers have horribly frightened."

Zourine went out into the street to excuse himself to Marie, and explain the mistake, and ordered the officer to place her and her maid in the best house in the city. I stayed with him. After supper, as soon as we were alone, I gave him the story of my adventures.

He shook his head. "That's all very well; but why will you marry? As an officer and a comrade, I tell you marriage is folly! Now listen to me. The road to Simbirsk has been swept clean by our soldiers; you can therefore send the Captain's daughter to your parents tomorrow, and remain yourself in my detachment. No need to return to Orenbourg; you might fall again into the hands of the rebels."

I resolved to follow, in part, Zourine's advice. Saveliitch came to prepare my room for the night. I told him to be ready to set out in the morning with Marie.

"Who will attend you, my lord?"

"My old friend," said I, trying to soften him, "I do not

need a servant here, and in serving Marie, you serve me, for I shall marry her as soon as the war is over."

"Marry!" repeated he, with his hands crossed, and a look of inexpressible blankness, "the child wants to marry! What will your parents say?"

"They will, no doubt, consent as soon as they know Marie. You will intercede for us, will you not?"

I had touched the old man's heart. "O Peter!" said he, "you are too young to marry, but the young lady is an angel, and it would be a sin to let the chance slip. I will do as you desire."

The next day I made known my plans to Marie. As Zourine's detachment was to leave the city that same day, delay was impossible. I confided Marie to my dear old Saveliitch, and gave him a letter for my father. Marie, in tears, took leave of me. I did not dare to speak, lest the bystanders should observe my feelings.

It was the end of the February; Winter, which had rendered manoeuvering difficult was now at a close, and our generals were preparing for a combined campaign. At the approach of our troops, revolted villages returned to their duty, while Prince Galitzin defeated the usurper, and raised the siege of Orenbourg, which was the death-blow to the rebellion. We heard of Pougatcheff in the Ural regions, and on the way to Moscow. But he was captured. The war was over. Zourine received orders to return his troops to their posts. I jumped about the room like a boy. Zourine shrugged his shoulders, and said: "Wait till you are married, and see how foolish you are!"

I had leave of absence. In a few days I would be at home

and united to Marie. One day Zourine came into my room with a paper in his hand, and sent away the servant.

"What's the matter?" said I.

"A slight annoyance," he answered, handing me the paper. "Read."

It was confidential order addressed to all the chiefs of detachments to arrest me, and send me under guard to Khasan before the Commission of Inquiry, created to give information against Pougatcheff and his accomplices. The paper fell from my hands.

"Do not be cast down," said Zourine, "but set out at once."

My conscience was easy, but the delay! It would be months, perhaps, before I could get through the Commission. Zourine bade me an affectionate adieu. I mounted the telega (Summer carriage), two hussars withdrawn swords beside, and took the road to Khasan.

Alexander Pushkin

XIV

THE SENTENCE

I had no doubt that I was arrested for having left the fortress of Orenbourg without leave, and felt sure that I could exculpate myself. Not only were we not forbidden, but on the contrary, we were encouraged to make forays against the enemy. My friendly relations with Pougatcheff, however, wore a suspicious look.

Arriving at Khasan, I found the city almost reduced to ashes. Along the streets there were heaps of calcined material of unroofed walls of houses—a proof that Pougatcheff had been there. The fortress was intact. I was taken there and delivered to the officer on duty. He ordered the blacksmith to rivet securely iron shackles on my feet. I was then consigned to a small, dark dungeon, lighted only by a loop- hole, barred with iron. This did not presage anything good, yet I did not lose courage; for, having tasted the delight of prayer, offered by a heart full of anguish, I fell asleep, without a thought for the morrow. The next morning I was taken before the Commission. Two soldiers crossed the yard with me, to the Commandant's dwelling. Stopping in the antechamber, they let me proceed alone to the interior.

I entered quite a spacious room. At a table, covered with papers, sat tow personages,—a General advanced in years, of stern aspect, and a young officer of the Guards, of easy and agreeable manners. Near the window, at another table, a secretary, pen on ear, bending over a paper, was ready to take my deposition.

The interrogation began: "Your name and profession?" The General asked if I was the son of Andrew Grineff, and upon my replying in the affirmative, exclaimed: "It is a pity so honorable a man should have a son so unworthy of him!"

I replied that I hoped to refute all charges against me, by a sincere avowal of the truth. My assurance displeased him.

"You are a bold fellow," said he, frowning; "but we have seen others like you."

The young officer asked how, and for what purpose I had entered the rebel service.

I replied indignantly, that being an officer and a noble, I was incapable of enlisting in the usurper's army, and had never served him in any way.

"How is it," said my judge, "that the 'officer and noble' is the only one spared by Pougatcheff? How is it that the 'officer and noble' received presents from the chief rebel, of a horse and a pelisse? Upon what is this intimacy founded, if not on treason, or at least unpardonable cowardice?"

The words wounded me, and I undertook with warmth my own defense, finally invoking the name of my General who could testify to my zeal during the siege of

Alexander Pushkin

Orenbourg. The severe old man took from the table an open letter, and read:

* * * "With regard to Ensign Griness, I have the honor to declare, that he was in the service at Orenbourg from the month of October, 1773, till the following February. Since then, he has not presented himself." * * *

Here the General said harshly: "What can you say now to justify your conduct?"

My judges had listened with interest and even kindness, to the recital of my acquaintance with the usurper, from the meeting in the snowdrift to the taking of Belogorsk, where he gave me my life through gratitude. I was going to continue my defense, by relating frankly my relations with Marie, and her rescue. But if I spoke of her the Commission would force her to appear, and her name would become the theme of no very delicate remarks by the interrogated witnesses. These thoughts so troubled me that I stammered, and at last was silent.

The judges were prejudiced against me by my evident confusion. The young Guardsman asked that I should be confronted by my chief accuser. Some minutes later the clank of iron fetters resounded, and Alexis entered.

He was pale and thin. His hair, formerly black as a raven's wing, was turning gray. He repeated his accusation in a weak but decided tone.

According to him, I was Pougatcheff's spy. I heard him to the end in silence, and rejoiced at one thing: he never pronounced the name of Marie Mironoff. Was it that his self-love smarted from her contemptuous rejection of him? or was there in his heart a spark of that same feeling which made me also silent on that point? This confirmed me in my resolution, and when asked what I had to answer to the charges of Alexis, I merely said that I held to my first declaration, and had nothing more to add.

The General remanded us to prison. I looked at Alexis. He smiled with satisfied hate, raised up his shackles to hasten his pace and pass before me. I had no further examination. I was not an eye-witness of what remains to be told the reader; but I have so often heard the story, that the minutest particulars are engraved on my memory.

Marie was received by my parents with the cordial courtesy which distinguished the preceding generation. They became very much attached to her, and my father no longer considered my love a folly. The news of my arrest was a fearful blow; but Marie and Saveliitch had so frankly told the origin of my connection with Pougatcheff, that the news did not seem grave. My father could not be persuaded that I would take part in an infamous revolt, whose object was the subversion of the throne and the extinction of the nobility. So better news was expected, and several weeks passed, when at last a letter came from our relative Prince B——. After the usual compliments, he told my father that the suspicions of my complicity in the rebel plots were only too well founded, as had been proved,—that an exemplary execution might have been my fate, were it not that the Empress, out of consideration for the father's white hair and loyal services, had commuted the sentence of the criminal son. She had exiled him for life to the depths of Siberia!

The blow nearly killed my father. his firmness gave way, and his usually silent sorrow burst into bitter plaints: "What! my son plotting with Pougatcheff! The Empress gives him his life! Execution not the worst thing in the world! My grandfather died on the scaffold in defense of his convictions! But, that a noble should betray his oath, unite with bandits, knaves and revolted slaves! shame! shame forever on our face!"

Frightened by his despair, my mother did not dare to show her grief, and Marie was more desolate than they. Persuaded that I could justify myself if I chose, she divined the motive of my silence, and believed that she was the cause of my suffering.

One evening, seated on his sofa, my father was turning over the leaves of the "*Court Almanac*," but his thoughts were far away, and the book did not produce its usual effect upon him. My mother was knitting in silence, and from time to time a furtive tear dropped upon her work. Marie, who was sewing in the same room, without any prelude declared to my parents that she was obliged to go to St. Petersburg, and begged them to furnish her the means.

My mother said: "Why will you leave us?"

Marie replied that her fate depended on this journey; that she was going to claim the protection of those in favor at Court, as the daughter of a man who had perished a victim to his loyalty.

My father bowed his head. A word which recalled the supposed crime of his son, seemed a sharp reproach.

"Go," said he, at last, with a sigh; "we will not place an obstacle to your happiness. May God give you an honorable husband and not a traitor!"

He rose and left the room. Alone with my mother, Marie confided to her, in part, the object of her journey. My mother, in tears, kissed her and prayed for the success of the project. A few days after, Marie, Polacca and Saveliitch left home.

When Marie reached Sofia, she learned that the Court was at that moment in residence at the summer palace of Tzarskoie-Selo. She decided to stop there, and obtained a small room at the post-house. The post mistress came to chat with the new-comer. She told Marie, pompously, that she was the niece of an official attached to the Court—her uncle having the honor of attending to the fires in her Majesty's abode! Marie soon knew at what hour the Empress rose, took her coffee, and went on the promenade; in brief, the conversation of Anna was like a page from the memoirs of the times, and would be very precious in our days. The two women went together to the Imperial gardens, where Anna told Marie the romance of each pathway and the history of every bridge over the artificial streams. Next day very early Marie returned alone to the Imperial gardens. The weather was superb. The sun gilded the linden tops, already seared by the Autumn frosts. The broad lake sparkled, the swans, just aroused, came out gravely from the shore. Marie was going to a charming green sward, when a little dog, of English blood, came running to her barking. She was startled; but a voice of rare refinement said: "He will not bite you; do not be afraid."

A lady about fifty years of age was seated on a rustic bench. She was dressed in a white morning-dress, a light cap and a mantilla. Her face, full and florid, was expressive of calmness and seriousness. She was the first to speak: "You are evidently a stranger here?"

"That is true, madam. I arrived from the country yesterday."

Alexander Pushkin

"You are with your parents?"

"No, madam, alone."

"You are too young to travel alone. Are you here on business?"

"My parents are dead. I came to present a petition to the Empress."

"You are an orphan; you have to complain of injustice, or injury?"

"Madam, I came to ask for a pardon, not justice."

"Permit me a question: Who are you?"

"I am the daughter of Captain Mironoff."

"Of Captain Mironoff? of him who commanded one of the fortresses in the province of Orenbourg?"

"The same, madam."

The lady seemed touched. "Pardon me, I am going to Court. Explain the object of your petition; perhaps I can aid you." Marie took from her pocket a paper which she handed to the lady, who read it attentively. Marie, whose eyes followed every movement of her countenance, was alarmed by the severe expression of face so calm and gracious a moment before.

"You intercede for Grineff?" said the lady, in an icy tone. "The Empress can not pardon him. He went over to the usurper, not as an ignorant believer, but as a depraved and dangerous good-for-nothing."

"It is not true!" exclaimed Marie.

"What! not true?" said the lady, flushing to the eyes.

"Before God, it is not true. I know all. I will tell you all. It was for me only that exposed himself to all these misfortunes. If he did not clear himself before his judges, it was because he would not drag me before the authorities." Marie then related with warmth all that the reader knows.

"Where do you lodge?" asked the lady, when the young girl had finished her recital. Upon hearing that she was staying with the postmaster's wife, she nodded, and said with a smile: "Ah! I know her. Adieu! tell no one of our meeting. I hope you will not have long to wait for the answer to your petition."

She rose and went away by a covered path. Marie went back to Anna's, full of fair hope. The postmaster's wife was surprised that Marie took so early a promenade, which might in Autumn, prove injurious to a young girl's health. She brought the *Somovar*, and with her cup of tea was going to relate one of her interminable stories, when a carriage with the imperial escutcheon stopped before the door. A lackey, wearing the imperial livery, entered and announced that her Majesty deigned to order to her presence the daughter of Captain Mironoff!

"Ah!" exclaimed Anna, "the Empress orders you to Court! How did she know you were with me? You can not present yourself—you do not know how to walk in courtly fashion! I ought to go with you. Shall I not send to the doctor's wife and get her yellow dress with flounces, for you?"

The lackey declared that he had orders to take Marie

Alexander Pushkin

alone, just as she was. Anna did not dare to disobey, and Marie set out. She had a presentiment that her destiny was now to be decided. Her heart beat violently. In a few minutes the carriage was at the palace, and Marie, having crossed a long suite of apartments, vacant and sumptuous, entered the *boudoir* of the Empress. The nobles who surrounded their sovereign respectfully made way for the young girl.

The Empress, in whom Marie recognized the lady of the garden, said, graciously: "I am pleased to be able to grant your prayer. Convinced of the innocence of your betrothed, I have arranged everything. Here is a letter for your future father-in-law."

Marie, in tears, fell at the feet of the Empress, who raised her up and kissed her, saying:

"I know that you are not rich; but I have to acquit myself of a debt to the daughter of a brave man, Captain Mironoff." Treating Marie with tenderness, the Empress dismissed her. That day Marie set out for my father's country-seat, not having even glanced at Saint Petersburg.

Here terminate the memoirs of Peter Grineff. We know by family tradition that he was set free about the end of the year 1774. We know too, that he was present at the execution of Pougatcheff, who, recognizing him in the crowd, gave him one last sign with the head which, a moment after, was shown to the people, bleeding and inanimate.

Peter Grineff became the husband of Marie Mironoff. Their descendents still live, in the Province of Simbirsk, and in the hereditary manor is still shown the autograph letter of the Empress Catherine II. It is addressed to

Andrew Grineff, and contains, with his son's justification, a touching and beautiful eulogium of Marie, the Captain's daughter.

ABOUT THE AUTHOR

Alexander Sergeyevich Pushkin (June 6 [O.S. May 26] 1799 – February 10 [O.S. January 29] 1837) was a Russian Romantic author who is considered to be the greatest Russian poet and the founder of modern Russian literature. Pushkin pioneered the use of vernacular speech in his poems and plays, creating a style of storytelling—mixing drama, romance, and satire—associated with Russian literature ever since and greatly influencing later Russian writers.

Born in Moscow, Pushkin published his first poem at the age of fifteen, and was widely recognized by the literary establishment by the time of his graduation from the Imperial Lyceum in Tsarskoe Selo. Pushkin gradually became committed to social reform and emerged as a spokesman for literary radicals; in the early 1820s he clashed with the government, which sent him into exile in southern Russia. While under the strict surveillance of government censors and unable to travel or publish at will, he wrote his most famous play, the drama Boris Godunov, but could not publish it until years later.

Pushkin and his wife Natalya Goncharova, whom he married in 1831, later became regulars of court society. In 1837, while falling into greater and greater debt amidst rumors that his wife had started conducting a scandalous affair, Pushkin challenged her alleged lover, Georges d'Anthès, to a duel. Pushkin was mortally wounded and died two days later.

Choose from Thousands of 1stWorldLibrary Classics By

A. M. Barnard
Ada Leverson
Adolphus William Ward
Aesop
Agatha Christie
Alexander Aaronsohn
Alexander Kielland
Alexandre Dumas
Alfred Gatty
Alfred Ollivant
Alice Duer Miller
Alice Turner Curtis
Alice Dunbar
Allen Chapman
Alleyne Ireland
Ambrose Bierce
Amelia E. Barr
Amory H. Bradford
Andrew Lang
Andrew McFarland Davis
Andy Adams
Angela Brazil
Anna Alice Chapin
Anna Sewell
Annie Besant
Annie Hamilton Donnell
Annie Payson Call
Annie Roe Carr
Annonaymous
Anton Chekhov
Archibald Lee Fletcher
Arnold Bennett
Arthur C. Benson
Arthur Conan Doyle
Arthur M. Winfield
Arthur Ransome
Arthur Schnitzler
Arthur Train
Atticus
B.H. Baden-Powell
B. M. Bower
B. C. Chatterjee
Baroness Emmuska Orczy
Baroness Orczy
Basil King
Bayard Taylor
Ben Macomber
Bertha Muzzy Bower
Bjornstjerne Bjornson

Booth Tarkington
Boyd Cable
Bram Stoker
C. Collodi
C. E. Orr
C. M. Ingleby
Carolyn Wells
Catherine Parr Traill
Charles A. Eastman
Charles Amory Beach
Charles Dickens
Charles Dudley Warner
Charles Farrar Browne
Charles Ives
Charles Kingsley
Charles Klein
Charles Hanson Towne
Charles Lathrop Pack
Charles Romyn Dake
Charles Whibley
Charles Willing Beale
Charlotte M. Braeme
Charlotte M. Yonge
Charlotte Perkins Stetson
Clair W. Hayes
Clarence Day Jr.
Clarence E. Mulford
Clemence Housman
Confucius
Coningsby Dawson
Cornelis DeWitt Wilcox
Cyril Burleigh
D. H. Lawrence
Daniel Defoe
David Garnett
Dinah Craik
Don Carlos Janes
Donald Keyhoe
Dorothy Kilner
Dougan Clark
Douglas Fairbanks
E. Nesbit
E. P. Roe
E. Phillips Oppenheim
E. S. Brooks
Earl Barnes
Edgar Rice Burroughs
Edith Van Dyne
Edith Wharton

Edward Everett Hale
Edward J. O'Biren
Edward S. Ellis
Edwin L. Arnold
Eleanor Atkins
Eleanor Hallowell Abbott
Eliot Gregory
Elizabeth Gaskell
Elizabeth McCracken
Elizabeth Von Arnim
Ellem Key
Emerson Hough
Emilie F. Carlen
Emily Bronte
Emily Dickinson
Enid Bagnold
Enilor Macartney Lane
Erasmus W. Jones
Ernie Howard Pie
Ethel May Dell
Ethel Turner
Ethel Watts Mumford
Eugene Sue
Eugenie Foa
Eugene Wood
Eustace Hale Ball
Evelyn Everett-green
Everard Cotes
F. H. Cheley
F. J. Cross
F. Marion Crawford
Fannie E. Newberry
Federick Austin Ogg
Ferdinand Ossendowski
Fergus Hume
Florence A. Kilpatrick
Fremont B. Deering
Francis Bacon
Francis Darwin
Frances Hodgson Burnett
Frances Parkinson Keyes
Frank Gee Patchin
Frank Harris
Frank Jewett Mather
Frank L. Packard
Frank V. Webster
Frederic Stewart Isham
Frederick Trevor Hill
Frederick Winslow Taylor

Friedrich Kerst
Friedrich Nietzsche
Fyodor Dostoyevsky
G.A. Henty
G.K. Chesterton
Gabrielle E. Jackson
Garrett P. Serviss
Gaston Leroux
George A. Warren
George Ade
Geroge Bernard Shaw
George Cary Eggleston
George Durston
George Ebers
George Eliot
George Gissing
George MacDonald
George Meredith
George Orwell
George Sylvester Viereck
George Tucker
George W. Cable
George Wharton James
Gertrude Atherton
Gordon Casserly
Grace E. King
Grace Gallatin
Grace Greenwood
Grant Allen
Guillermo A. Sherwell
Gulielma Zollinger
Gustav Flaubert
H. A. Cody
H. B. Irving
H. C. Bailey
H. G. Wells
H. H. Munro
H. Irving Hancock
H. R. Naylor
H. Rider Haggard
H. W. C. Davis
Haldeman Julius
Hall Caine
Hamilton Wright Mabie
Hans Christian Andersen
Harold Avery
Harold McGrath
Harriet Beecher Stowe
Harry Castlemon
Harry Coghill
Harry Houidini

Hayden Carruth
Helent Hunt Jackson
Helen Nicolay
Hendrik Conscience
Hendy David Thoreau
Henri Barbusse
Henrik Ibsen
Henry Adams
Henry Ford
Henry Frost
Henry James
Henry Jones Ford
Henry Seton Merriman
Henry W Longfellow
Herbert A. Giles
Herbert Carter
Herbert N. Casson
Herman Hesse
Hildegard G. Frey
Homer
Honore De Balzac
Horace B. Day
Horace Walpole
Horatio Alger Jr.
Howard Pyle
Howard R. Garis
Hugh Lofting
Hugh Walpole
Humphry Ward
Ian Maclaren
Inez Haynes Gillmore
Irving Bacheller
Isabel Cecilia Williams
Isabel Hornibrook
Israel Abrahams
Ivan Turgenev
J. G.Austin
J. Henri Fabre
J. M. Barrie
J. M. Walsh
J. Macdonald Oxley
J. R. Miller
J. S. Fletcher
J. S. Knowles
J. Storer Clouston
J. W. Duffield
Jack London
Jacob Abbott
James Allen
James Andrews
James Baldwin

James Branch Cabell
James DeMille
James Joyce
James Lane Allen
James Lane Allen
James Oliver Curwood
James Oppenheim
James Otis
James R. Driscoll
Jane Abbott
Jane Austen
Jane L. Stewart
Janet Aldridge
Jens Peter Jacobsen
Jerome K. Jerome
Jessie Graham Flower
John Buchan
John Burroughs
John Cournos
John F. Kennedy
John Gay
John Glasworthy
John Habberton
John Joy Bell
John Kendrick Bangs
John Milton
John Philip Sousa
John Taintor Foote
Jonas Lauritz Idemil Lie
Jonathan Swift
Joseph A. Altsheler
Joseph Carey
Joseph Conrad
Joseph E. Badger Jr
Joseph Hergesheimer
Joseph Jacobs
Jules Vernes
Julian Hawthrone
Julie A Lippmann
Justin Huntly McCarthy
Kakuzo Okakura
Karle Wilson Baker
Kate Chopin
Kenneth Grahame
Kenneth McGaffey
Kate Langley Bosher
Kate Langley Bosher
Katherine Cecil Thurston
Katherine Stokes
L. A. Abbot
L. T. Meade

L. Frank Baum
Latta Griswold
Laura Dent Crane
Laura Lee Hope
Laurence Housman
Lawrence Beasley
Leo Tolstoy
Leonid Andreyev
Lewis Carroll
Lewis Sperry Chafer
Lilian Bell
Lloyd Osbourne
Louis Hughes
Louis Joseph Vance
Louis Tracy
Louisa May Alcott
Lucy Fitch Perkins
Lucy Maud Montgomery
Luther Benson
Lydia Miller Middleton
Lyndon Orr
M. Corvus
M. H. Adams
Margaret E. Sangster
Margret Howth
Margaret Vandercook
Margaret W. Hungerford
Margret Penrose
Maria Edgeworth
Maria Thompson Daviess
Mariano Azuela
Marion Polk Angellotti
Mark Overton
Mark Twain
Mary Austin
Mary Catherine Crowley
Mary Cole
Mary Hastings Bradley
Mary Roberts Rinehart
Mary Rowlandson
M. Wollstonecraft Shelley
Maud Lindsay
Max Beerbohm
Myra Kelly
Nathaniel Hawthrone
Nicolo Machiavelli
O. F. Walton
Oscar Wilde
Owen Johnson
P.G. Wodehouse
Paul and Mabel Thorne

Paul G. Tomlinson
Paul Severing
Percy Brebner
Percy Keese Fitzhugh
Peter B. Kyne
Plato
Quincy Allen
R. Derby Holmes
R. L. Stevenson
R. S. Ball
Rabindranath Tagore
Rahul Alvares
Ralph Bonehill
Ralph Henry Barbour
Ralph Victor
Ralph Waldo Emmerson
Rene Descartes
Ray Cummings
Rex Beach
Rex E. Beach
Richard Harding Davis
Richard Jefferies
Richard Le Gallienne
Robert Barr
Robert Frost
Robert Gordon Anderson
Robert L. Drake
Robert Lansing
Robert Lynd
Robert Michael Ballantyne
Robert W. Chambers
Rosa Nouchette Carey
Rudyard Kipling
Saint Augustine
Samuel B. Allison
Samuel Hopkins Adams
Sarah Bernhardt
Sarah C. Hallowell
Selma Lagerlof
Sherwood Anderson
Sigmund Freud
Standish O'Grady
Stanley Weyman
Stella Benson
Stella M. Francis
Stephen Crane
Stewart Edward White
Stijn Streuvels
Swami Abhedananda
Swami Parmananda
T. S. Ackland

T. S. Arthur
The Princess Der Ling
Thomas A. Janvier
Thomas A Kempis
Thomas Anderton
Thomas Bailey Aldrich
Thomas Bulfinch
Thomas De Quincey
Thomas Dixon
Thomas H. Huxley
Thomas Hardy
Thomas More
Thornton W. Burgess
U. S. Grant
Upton Sinclair
Valentine Williams
Various Authors
Vaughan Kester
Victor Appleton
Victor G. Durham
Victoria Cross
Virginia Woolf
Wadsworth Camp
Walter Camp
Walter Scott
Washington Irving
Wilbur Lawton
Wilkie Collins
Willa Cather
Willard F. Baker
William Dean Howells
William le Queux
W. Makepeace Thackeray
William W. Walter
William Shakespeare
Winston Churchill
Yei Theodora Ozaki
Yogi Ramacharaka
Young E. Allison
Zane Grey

www.ingramcontent.com/pod-product-compliance
Lightning Source LLC
Chambersburg PA
CBHW051851170626
46807CB00003B/1433